PRAISE FOR USA TODAY BESTSELLING AUTHOR
JAN MORAN

The Winemakers

"Readers will devour this page-turner as the mystery and passions spin out." – *Library Journal*

"As she did in *Scent of Triumph*, Moran weaves knowledge of wine and winemaking into this intense family drama." – *Booklist*

"Jan Moran is the new queen of the epic romance." — Rebecca Forster, *USA Today* Bestselling Author

The Chocolatier and *Scent of Triumph*

"A delicious novel, makes you long for chocolate." – *Ciao Tutti*

"A wonderful, smoothly written novel. Full of intrigue, love, secrets, and romance." – *Lekker Lezen*

"*Scent of Triumph* is a captivating tale of love, determination and reinvention." — Karen Marin, Givenchy Paris

Seabreeze Inn and *Coral Cottage* series

"The women are intelligent and strong. At the core of Jan's books is a strong, close-knit family." — Betty's Reviews

BOOKS BY JAN MORAN

20th-Century Historical

Hepburn's Necklace

The Chocolatiers

The Winemakers: A Novel of Wine and Secrets

Scent of Triumph: A Novel of Perfume and Passion

Life is a Cabernet: A Wine Novella

Contemporary

Coral Cottage

Coral Cafe

Seabreeze Inn

Seabreeze Summer

Seabreeze Sunset

A Seabreeze Inn Christmas

Flawless

Beauty Mark

Runway

Essence

Style

Sparkle

LIFE IS A CABERNET

A WINE COUNTRY NOVELLA

JAN MORAN

SUNNY PALMS

PRESS

Library of Congress Cataloging-in-Publication Data
Moran, Jan.
/ by Jan Moran
ISBN 978-1-942073-63-5 (softcover)
ISBN 9781942073628 (epub)

9663 Santa Monica Blvd STE 1158
Beverly Hills, CA, USA
www.JanMoran.com

CHAPTER 1

*S*an Francisco, Summer, 1956

"Look at the life in this cabernet." Henri Laurent held an etched glass aloft to catch the sun's fleeting rays slanting through the window. The wine glass cast multicolored prisms across his serious expression, while the dark, ruby-colored wine shimmered with vitality. "The more stress placed upon the vine, the better the wine. These grapes are the survivors, the finest and strongest nature can offer. Try it with me now."

While Henri pursed his lips to taste the wine, Juliana Cardona was as transfixed as the rest of the crowd she'd gathered on this cool summer afternoon in San Francisco at the tony St. Francis Hotel. The winemaker's mesmerizing delivery had captured the attention of every female journalist in the room she'd booked for the press party. Though greatly outnumbered by their male counterparts, women more often influenced the selection of wines at the city's most high-profile parties on Nob Hill.

Juliana turned to the fashionably dressed executive editor seated next to her in the front row. "Bessie, which one is your favorite?"

The woman tilted her head toward Henri, whose passion for wine was transmuted into graceful, even sensual, movements. "Definitely this one."

"You haven't even tasted the wine."

"Oh, were you talking about the wine?" Bessie sighed and sipped from her tasting glass. "Mmm, as delightful as the vintner. How were you able to get him here? He's been the mystery man of Napa Valley."

"I have my ways." Juliana winked at her. In truth, he'd been the most difficult winemaker to engage in her promotion for Northern California wines, which was underwritten by Napa and Sonoma wineries. This event was the first one of its kind she had planned and she'd been nervous about every detail.

Only Raphael Casini, who managed the vineyards at the well-respected Mille Étoiles vineyards where she had grown up, had been able to persuade Henri to appear. She didn't ask Raphael how he'd managed that.

Ever since Henri Laurent and his family had acquired the old vineyards and winery in Calistoga a few years ago, there had been talk. The Laurent family kept to themselves, which only fueled speculation. Rumors spread that they had wired large sums of money to the bank and were using methods unlike any other winemakers in the valley. The grape pickers spoke of abundant harvests, yet few Chateau Laurent wines had been released.

"He's a strange one, though," Bessie continued. "I've contacted Henri in the past to feature him, but he always declines and offers no explanation."

That *was* curious, Juliana agreed. Most winemakers

would welcome a feature article in *Wine Appreciation*, the wine industry's most prestigious publication. Bessie and her husband, Gilbert Waters, had catapulted several wineries to success through their coverage. Every wine collector and luxury hotelier read the magazine. Why wouldn't he want an article on his wine? And he was certainly a handsome representative.

A reporter raised his hand to Henri. "You said you're using new methods in winemaking, such as malolactic fermentation. Can you explain that?"

"That's the process of turning malic acid into lactic acid," Henri said. "It uses bacteria rather than yeast. In short, malolactic fermentation results in a smoother, rounder taste on the palate. This method is used more in Europe. You'll find more information on the handout provided for you."

Juliana closed her eyes for a moment, listening to the sound of Henri's deep voice. It was as smooth and rich as the wines he created. He was an American, but certain words carried a slightly different accent as if he might have spoken French in years past. His surname was French, and he advocated European winemaking methods, but beyond that, she knew little of the man. Nor did anyone else.

Bessie held a white-gloved hand to her red lipstick-painted mouth and whispered, "Have you heard if he's seeing anyone?"

Juliana shook her head. "His wife hasn't been gone long." That question cut close to her heart. She braced herself for what was surely coming next. Waiting, she picked at a thread on the new burgundy-colored suit she'd bought especially for this event.

"She died a year ago. A handsome man like that with two small children? He's sure to marry someone soon."

Bessie's face lit. "You two have a lot in common, seeing as how Alfonso is, well… no longer with us, poor boy." She patted Juliana's shoulder in sympathy. "I'm so sorry, dear, but you're still a young woman. A man that virile would probably give you babies, too."

Blinking back a sudden sting behind her eyes, Juliana offered a polite smile, though the muscles in her jaw tightened reflexively. She and Alfonso Villareal had known each other from childhood and had dated for years. Everyone assumed they would marry. She did, too.

Juliana still remembered the day Alfonso had joined the Army to work in military intelligence. He'd been so proud of representing his country and had looked so handsome in his uniform. He was excited about serving in Korea. After graduating from high school, she had waited four more interminable years, going to college while he was gone. As Alfonso's time in the service drew to a close, they were ecstatic, their dreams in sight.

The wedding was planned, she'd made her dress, and their families were looking forward to welcoming him home. And then, just a week before he was to leave Korea, he was killed in a military ambush.

Inside, Juliana's heart was still raw. Alfonso's death might as well have happened yesterday, rather than five years ago. She could only imagine how difficult life must be for Henri, who had two children to look after, though he seemed like a thoughtful, patient man.

Winemakers had to have an abundance of patience. It took years from the time new rootstock was planted, and vines bore fruit, until the wine was sufficiently aged in barrels before bottling. Many of the original vines in the valley had withered long ago. The number of vineyards had been significantly depleted during Prohibition, which had wiped out the majority of grape farmers and wine-makers during the 1920s and 1930s. It hadn't been until after the depression and the Second World War that the industry had started to grow again. Juliana couldn't be more excited.

A new era of winemaking was underway in the United States, and opportunities abounded. So why was Henri so serious in his delivery? But then, with his voice, he could probably read the telephone book and draw a crowd of admirers.

When Henri finished, Juliana rose and addressed the gathering of press and vintners. "Thank you all for coming today. We have so many incredible wines being produced today in our region, wines that can stand on the world stage in terms of excellence." This she knew from her childhood friend Caterina Rosetta, who was a sommelier at the St. Francis Hotel and had access to the world's finest wines. She also had one of the best wine palates in the valley.

Juliana went on. "I'd like to thank my friends and colleagues at Chateau Laurent, Mille Étoiles, and Beringer, as well as those at Charles Krug, Inglenook, Gundlach Bundschu, and Buena Vista. For our press guests, we invite you to stay and enjoy the wine. Please don't hesitate to ask questions, because that's why our winemakers are here. Cheers," she added, raising her glass of Chateau Laurent, though she'd only taken a sip.

Amid the polite applause, Juliana surveyed the high-ceilinged, wainscoted meeting room to make sure people were meeting and mingling. She saw Caterina and her mother, Ava Rosetta, who was the stylish winemaker and proprietor of Mille Étoiles winery, at the rear of the room talking to a San Francisco newspaper reporter. Bessie was speaking to Raphael Casini, who was an expert in viticulture and Ava's *vigneron* from Montalcino, Italy. Gilbert was asking them to pose for a photograph. Juliana turned to find Henri.

To her dismay, Henri was putting on his hat.

"Excuse me, Mr. Laurent. May I have a word with you?" Juliana hurried toward him. She didn't want the winemakers to start leaving, because she'd promised her press contacts access to them. Henri didn't pause until he was at the door. She saw his shoulders rise and drop, and then he turned reluctantly to her.

"Yes?" Henri still had on his hat.

"I wanted to thank you for coming." Juliana fumbled for something to say. His dark eyebrows framed cognac-colored eyes that immediately swept her under his spell.

"My pleasure." He nodded curtly and began to turn.

"Gilbert and Bessie Waters of *Wine Appreciation* magazine would like to speak to you." Juliana pressed her palms together.

Slowly, he removed his hat and looked over his shoulder.

"They'd like photographs of all the winemakers together." Juliana waved at Gilbert.

"No photos." Henri put his hat back on to leave.

"Wait," Juliana said, touching the sleeve of his light wool jacket. "There's something else I'd like to ask you."

Henri's gaze slid to her hand, which was now resting on his forearm. Before Juliana could pull her hand away, he placed his hand on hers. "What is it, Miss Cardona?"

She lowered her eyes to his elegant, tapered fingers resting on hers. His skin was smooth, so unlike other farmer's hands. "Please call me Juliana."

"Juliana."

At the sound of her name on his lips, Juliana was

rendered nearly breathless. "I—I'm wondering where you sell your wine." She edged her hand away, hoping he didn't feel it quivering.

Finally, a smile tugged on one side of his mouth. "I haven't sold any in a few years."

"But why not?"

His eyes darted to one side, and then he replied, "I suppose the wine is aging."

"Could I visit your home? I mean, could I see how you make your wines? The way you explained your process, you make it sound so interesting." Juliana stopped herself, wishing she could melt away. She'd just invited herself to this man's home. Where were her manners? Her mother would chastise her if she'd heard her. This was not the way she had been raised.

But she was a modern woman, not of her mother's generation. Juliana squared her shoulders and gave Henri a bright smile, as if asking to visit him was the most natural thing to do. "I have ideas that could help you promote your wines."

His eyes crinkled at the corners, signaling bemusement. "You're welcome to come anytime, Juliana. Will you come alone?"

"I might have a reporter with me. They're all so eager to speak to you."

He gazed out at the clutch of winemakers and reporters, who seemed relaxed, chatting and sipping wine. "Yes, I can see that." A smile touched his lips.

Juliana looked sheepishly through her dark lashes at him. "Well, maybe not this very moment."

He put his hand on her forearm, and she felt a jolt of energy course through her. "You are welcome with or without a chaperone." He chuckled.

"I'm not that young." Juliana was suddenly incensed. "Are you laughing at me?"

Henri just shook his head. "You're a gusty young woman, aren't you?"

Juliana glared at him. "You would be, too, if you were me. You men get to do exactly what you want. I started this publicity business because none of you in the wine industry would hire a woman. So yes, I have to be gutsy, as you put it, to do what I love and pay the rent." She stopped herself, touching her lips. Why couldn't she control her tongue?

Henri was looking at her with renewed interest. "Come by tomorrow at 11:00." Then he put his hat on and left.

Juliana groaned to herself. How could she have done such an embarrassing thing?

"Hey, why are you looking so glum?" Caterina tapped her on the shoulder.

Relieved to see her friend, Juliana said, "Oh, Cat, you have no idea what I just did."

"Besides put on a successful event? My mother has been talking to the society editor and the food editor at the *San Francisco Chronicle*. She'd like for you to help her with press coverage. Seems like your dream is coming true."

Caterina was right. Juliana had dreamed of having her own publicity business. She'd not only finished high school, but also college, quite a feat for an immigrant whose father had left her and her mother penniless. Her mother, Nina, worked as a cook for Caterina's family. Nina and Caterina's mother, Ava, had become close over the years after the death of Ava's husband and through the lean Depression years. Juliana shot a look at her friend. "I just invited myself to see Henri Laurent tomorrow."

"He might be a good client for you. What's so terrible about that?"

Juliana folded her arms. "He's disturbing, that's what he is."

"You just haven't dated anyone since Alfonso." With an understanding smile, Caterina handed Juliana a glass of wine and led her back to the crowd. "Come on, you have work to do. And wait until you hear about the new lead I have for you."

CHAPTER 2

*T*apping the steering wheel to the beat of Elvis Presley's "Don't Be Cruel" and singing at the top of her lungs, Juliana kicked up clouds of dust on the back roads of Calistoga. When she reached Chateau Laurent, she turned down the radio and wheeled her faded red Chevrolet Stylemaster into the entry. Towering eucalyptus trees that released a fresh minty menthol scent shielded the property from view.

Henri was waiting for her. He unlocked the nondescript wooden gate and waved her in. "Park in front of the house," he said, pointing to the right.

"Hop in. I'll take you back."

"Go on. I have to lock up."

"Most of us in the country don't even lock the house," Juliana said, but he only shrugged and closed the gate behind her. She wondered if he'd grown up in a city.

Juliana drove on and parked in front of an old stone Victorian-styled home that dated from the 1800s when the first vintners from Europe had arrived in the valley. She pushed in the parking brake with her high-heeled, leather spectator pump and then turned the rearview mirror toward her. As she touched up her matte red lipstick, she glanced in the mirror behind her. Henri was wearing a pinstriped shirt and burgundy silk tie with a buttoned vest over matching charcoal slacks. Hardly an outfit most vintners in the valley wore.

"Any trouble finding us?" Henri opened her car door for her.

"I grew up here. I know all the back roads." Brushing wrinkles from her navy cotton skirt, she slid out from the bench seat, holding a folder with notes she'd prepared in one hand and her purse in the other. She stood and gazed up at the fine old two-story structure. "This is one of the early wineries in the valley."

Henri shut the car door and stood beside her, hands on his hips. "The vineyard was planted in 1880, and the house was built about five years later. I've been restoring it since I bought it. Indoor plumbing was a must."

"You're not doing the work yourself, are you?"

"No, I hired several fine craftsmen from here via San Miguel de Allende." He looked quizzically at her. "How did you know?"

"You have the smoothest farmer's hands I've ever seen."

"I guess I do now." Henri turned his hands over as if inspecting them for the first time. "I have a vineyard manager, but I'm in charge of the winemaking. Come on, I'll show you around. And then I want to hear your proposal for my wine."

Juliana walked through the arched entry and gazed the around the comfortable room. Judging from the grand exterior, Juliana had thought the interior would be more formal. Bright-colored fabrics covered contemporary chairs and sofas, which lightened the dark wood floors and the wooden beamed ceiling high overhead. Light-infused Impressionist-style paintings hung on the walls, bringing pastoral scenes of nature indoors. "It's so modern inside. You have good taste." As soon as the words left her mouth, she wished she could have taken them back.

"Solange decorated this," Henri said quietly.

Moistening her lips, Juliana turned to him. "I'm so sorry for your loss. I didn't mean to bring it up." Her chest tightened as the memory of Alfonso came rushing back.

"It's all right. She'd been sick for a long time." Henri studied his shoes thoughtfully and then looked up. "You wanted to see the winery. Come, I'll show you."

Juliana followed him through the house. Once outside, they passed a trickling three-tiered fountain and crossed the lawn. He opened a heavy wooden door to a structure near a hillside, and then descended the stairway into a cellar. Juliana followed him down, her high heels tapping on each step. The sound echoed through the white plastered stairwell.

Henri gestured to the large room before them. "This is where we store the wine for aging."

Her eyes widening, Juliana swung around. The cellar was cool and smelled of musty aging wine, but it was a smell she loved. Everywhere she looked were barrels stacked high. Not just any barrels, but small ones of the finest French oak. She recognized them from Ava Rosetta's cave at Mille Étoiles. These were not often used in the valley, except by the most discriminating vintners. "You have quite an investment here. Why haven't you been bottling your wine?"

"Solange had been ill, though she was designing a new label when she died. She hadn't finished it."

Juliana understood the pain in his voice. "Then you

need a new label," she said softly. "I can help you with that."

They walked through an arched tunnel that led deeper into the cave, which had been carved into the hillside. Here the wine could rest undisturbed in cooler temperatures. Henri explained some of the new techniques he'd brought from Europe. He spoke of cold fermentation and the various levels of char on the inside of the barrels used for flavoring.

With his deep, rich voice, Juliana could have listened to him forever. She was familiar with a lot of what he said. Ava was from France, and she also insisted on the highest levels of quality.

As they were emerging from the cellar, Juliana asked where he was from.

"I'm from Boston."

"You have an interesting accent. I detect a slight French accent in some words."

Henri didn't respond at first. "I went to boarding school in Europe."

"In France?"

Another hesitation. "In Switzerland. I had French-speaking instructors."

"I'd love to visit Paris," Juliana said. "Did you ever go there?"

"I did." As if mired in the past, Henri fell silent.

Suddenly, Juliana felt like an idiot. Henri was perhaps ten years older than she was, which meant he'd probably served his country. "Were you in the war in Europe?"

"Yes," he said, but offered no details.

Just then, footsteps clattered in the hall as two little girls raced into the room. "Henri, Henri!" They stumbled and stopped when they saw Juliana, their mouths gaping.

Henri put an arm around each girl. "This is Beatrice, and this is Anne. Girls, meet Miss Juliana Cardona. Haven't I taught you how to greet a lady?"

Looking serious, the two girls held the edges of their pressed, cotton print dresses and bent their knees, dropping awkward curtseys. Juliana thought she would burst out laughing, but she didn't want to seem rude.

The girls were adorable. Dressed in a blue gingham dress, Anne was the taller of the two, with curly dark hair and big brown eyes. Beatrice was slighter in build and had blond hair and blue eyes. They hardly looked like sisters. Juliana imagined his wife must have had a fair complexion.

Smiling, Juliana curtsied back. "I'm happy to meet you."

The girls giggled, their eyes wide.

A pudgy aproned housekeeper appeared at the door to the living area. "Excuse me, Mr. Laurent, you have a telephone call."

"I'll only be a moment," he said to Juliana. He turned to the girls. "And you two, behave."

Seeing Henri as a father, Juliana was intrigued. She sat on a chair covered in yellow fabric, and the two girls sat on the light green sofa next to her. A small round table filled with family photos sat to one side. "I haven't seen you girls around town before."

Anne shot a look at Beatrice, who looked up at Juliana with a shy smile. "We don't go to town very often," Anne said.

"But we like to," Beatrice added.

The girls were so precious that Juliana could have smothered them with hugs. "What grades are you in at school?"

"Fifth," Anne said.

Beatrice shook her head. "Some of our books are for grades six and seven."

"That's English and math." Anne turned to Juliana. "We're eleven."

Beatrice pressed her hand against her mouth, giggling. "We're not in grade eleven. We're eleven years old."

Juliana smiled. "Both of you?"

"Yes, ma'am." They bounced on the sofa, their long hair swinging around their narrow shoulders.

"Where do you go to school?"

Anne stopped bouncing. "We go to school upstairs."

"We have a history lesson this afternoon," Beatrice said. "Our teacher comes after lunch."

"History was one of my favorite subjects." Juliana grinned at them. No wonder she hadn't seen the girls around. Many school children walked home past the boarding house in Napa where she lived. After Alfonso had died, she'd stayed on at her mother's cottage at Mille Étoiles for a little while. But it was lonely there without her childhood friends.

When Caterina graduated from the university, she'd taken an apartment in San Francisco. Santo, whose older cousin Raphael ran the vineyards at Mille Étoiles, had moved to Davis and started his own consulting business. Juliana had desperately needed a change. She moved into a respectable boarding house in Napa that rented only to single women.

The girls were telling Juliana more about their favorite subjects when Henri walked into the room. "I hope they've been nice," he said, looking from the girls to Juliana.

"They've been wonderful. They were just telling me about their studies and tutors. Did they ever go to school here?"

Henri stroked his chin. "It was better for them to learn at home."

"Of course," Juliana said. If their mother had been ill for a long time, she wouldn't have been able to drive them to school. They lived too far to walk to school. It seemed like an isolated life for two lively little girls.

Beatrice cupped her hands and whispered into Anne's ear.

Henri frowned. "What have I told you about telling secrets in front of other people?"

"It's rude." Beatrice pushed out her lower lip and raised her eyes to Juliana. "I'm sorry I was rude."

"Apology accepted." Juliana pressed her hand against her chest and tried to seem serious, but she found it nearly impossible.

"Very good, thank you, Beatrice. Now girls, Mrs. Peabody has a snack for you in the kitchen." Henri clapped his hands. "Time to go. Miss Cardona and I have business to discuss."

The two children stood. "It was a pleasure to meet you, Miss Cardona," Beatrice said, glancing to Henri for approval.

Henri nodded. "Anne?"

"Very, very, very nice to meet you." The little girl threw her arms around Juliana's neck. "We love you," Anne whispered.

Juliana hugged her back. "I have a lot of love in my heart for little girls like you, too."

Beatrice leaned in and cupped her hand around Juliana's ear, whispering, "Are you going to be our mother now?" Looking over her shoulder at Henri, Beatrice said, "It's not rude if I whisper to *her*."

Henri shook his head, hiding a grin behind his hand.

"I'm just a friend," Juliana whispered back. Wrapping an arm around each girl, she kissed them on the tops of their heads. "I think you're the sweetest, smartest girls I've met in a long, long time. I hope I see you again soon."

"So do we." The girls jumped up and down. "Can we see Miss Cardona again? Please?"

"Perhaps. Off with you two, now." Chuckling, Henri put his hands on their shoulders and guided them into the kitchen. The aroma of cooking wound through the doorway to the kitchen.

When Henri returned, Juliana said, "They're so cute, Henri. You must be proud of them."

Henri sat in a chair next to her and placed his hands on his knees. "I am, but they're a handful. What did Beatrice whisper to you?" He gazed at her with curiosity.

"Oh, it was just girl talk." Juliana smiled.

"They really took to you," he said with a note of amazement in his voice. "They're usually shy around new people."

Juliana had so many questions. Would it be rude to ask? She moistened her lips. "They said they're both eleven."

"Ah, yes." Henri rocked back in his chair. "They were born quite close together."

"That must have been a surprise."

"It certainly was, but things happen."

Why did she feel like he was hiding something? Juliana smoothed her skirt. Then again, what business was it of hers?

"You said you have some ideas for my wine business." Henri's golden amber eyes caught hers.

"Yes, I do." Returning his gaze, she realized that even her toes felt tingly when he looked at her. She reached for the folder she'd brought. Clearing her throat, she began.

"You've created exceptional wines, but few people know about them. I was glad you attended the wine and press event."

Henri snorted. "Raphael threatened to pick me up and take me there himself if I didn't."

"And how do you know Raphael?"

"I've seen him in town several times. He knew a lot about the history of my vineyard, so he approached me and made a few suggestions that proved helpful."

"I see." Her heart racing, Juliana crossed her legs and tried to appear calm. "Your cabernet sauvignon is one of the finest in the valley. The last few years must have been difficult for you and your children. It's understandable that your wine business has suffered, too. But that's where I can help you, Henri."

"It's probably time we expand our distribution." Henri clasped his hands. "That's what Solange wanted, but it's been difficult without her." He glanced at the photos on the table.

Juliana touched his hands. "Solange will always be part of Chateau Laurent wines. Do this in her memory and for your children. With or without me. What matters is that you embrace your passion for winemaking."

Henri shook his head. "Solange was my best friend."

"I felt the same way about Alfonso," she said quietly. "We told each other everything." Alfonso had been honest, loyal, and hard-working. They'd shared each other's dreams and goals from childhood.

"Were you married?" Henri's lips parted in surprise.

"Almost. We were engaged." Juliana told him about Alfonso, his military service in Korea, and the wedding they'd planned. Somehow, as she spoke about Alfonso to

Henri, her burden seemed lighter. "So you see, it's important to continue our lives. In so doing, we honor them."

"How do you figure that?"

"If Solange encouraged you and was proud of your accomplishments, then she shared the love you have for your talent. She would have wanted you to share it with others."

"Did Alfonso encourage you?" Instantly, Henri looked apologetic. "That is, if you don't mind my asking."

"I don't mind. You're easy to talk to." Juliana felt her face warm, but it was the truth. "Alfonso was so proud of me. He was confident enough in himself to shine a light on others. When I graduated from college, he was in the front row cheering for me. He used to brag about me to his friends. We would've had such a good life together." She paused, smiling. For the first time, it actually felt good talking about him.

"You still can." Henri rose and took her hand. "I like talking to you. Shall we continue over a glass of that cabernet you like so much?"

When Juliana hesitated, he said, "It's almost noon. Mrs. Peabody will have lunch for us."

He still held her hand, waiting.

"I'd like that very much." Juliana felt light-headed at his touch. Discussing her publicity plan for him over a glass of wine now seemed like an excellent idea.

CHAPTER 3

*H*enri couldn't believe his luck. Across from him sat a beautiful young woman. He raised a glass of cabernet he'd just drawn from a barrel. "To our new friendship." He'd ventured into dangerous new territory, but from what he'd seen, Juliana Cardona could be well worth it.

"A new friendship," she intoned.

A smile lit her dark brown eyes, melting his resolve. Henri brought the glass to his lips. Neither of them looked away as they took a sip.

Inhaling the bouquet, Juliana said, "Your wine is aging well."

"I'm pleased my experiments are working." Henri swirled his glass on the old oak table in the tasting room. Solange had insisted on preparing this room to receive visitors, but they'd never had a chance to use it because she tired so easily.

Henri chuckled to himself. "I'm glad you met Anne and Beatrice. That's the first chance they've had to perform their curtseys. You were a good sport."

"They're precious. You're so blessed to have them."

Juliana peered at her wine, assessing it with the ingrained habit of a native valley winemaker.

"We're lucky to have each other." For him and Solange, the babies had been pure lights in their lives, just when the world had seemed so dark. At first, he'd thought Solange had lost her mind, but after he'd held the first baby, he had fallen irrevocably in love with the helpless new life. "And you? As a career lady, do you want to have children someday?"

"I do. I wish I'd at least had a child with Alfonso. We'd thought about getting married while he was in the military, but we decided to wait."

"You're still young."

She laughed. "Not as young as you seem to think."

Her laughter was sweet music to his soul. Henri rested his chin in his hand, gazing at her. He'd been enchanted from the first moment he'd seen her at the St. Francis Hotel. She wore her silky dark hair brushed from her forehead and secured with a wide band. Her navy skirt nipped in at her tiny waist. Even with heels on, she was much shorter than he was. A perfume that smelled like warm, springtime jasmine wafted from her skin as she spoke, drawing him even closer to her. He leaned in, and then caught himself. Juliana was here on business; he had to respect that.

"Tell me about the ideas you have for Chateau Laurent wines," he said. When she'd mentioned visiting him here, he'd immediately taken her up on the idea, even though she'd seemed nervous about it. In truth, he was, too. On the way home, he'd vacillated between calling her and canceling, or inviting her to dinner instead.

Juliana brushed her hair over her shoulder and opened her folder. "As I mentioned, we'll need to finish designing your new label. Maybe we can use the design Solange started, or modify it."

"I think she'd like that." Solange had dreamed of being an artist like Mary Cassatt or Berthe Morisot, her favorite female Impressionist painters. Too weak to go out, she'd painted scenes from her window and her memory.

"To spread the word in San Francisco, I'd like to organize tastings with the city's most influential women. I've helped several of them stock wine cellars for their homes. These women—and couples—are serious wine collectors, and they're quite involved with charities."

Henri nodded, listening. "That's a good idea." He was impressed that she had such high-profile clients.

"Next, we'll court the press. I know reporters who write for several important newspapers on the west coast. A few have moved on to larger cities so we can reach Chicago and New York as well."

"I like that, too."

"I'm sure you know the wine industry publications. We can start with *Wine Appreciation* magazine. Bessie Waters is a friend, and she wants to talk to you. I can arrange an interview soon."

Henri shifted uneasily in his chair. "We'll see." Her husband had been intent on photographing him, but Henri had successfully dodged Gilbert Waters and his shiny Graflex Speed Graphic camera.

Juliana looked quizzical. "Does this have anything to do with why you didn't want your photo taken?" She paused and smiled. "Or were you just running away from me?"

"What can I say?" He attempted a laugh, but it came out strangled. Actually, he had been avoiding her. Juliana had unnerved him—he hadn't allowed himself to feel like this about a woman in years.

Juliana's manner softened. "I saw the family photographs in the living room."

Solange had been experimenting with photography, so Henri had relented, knowing these photographs would go no farther. He'd lived in the shadows for so long that this behavior was firmly entrenched. "Those were personal. For business, I'd rather the focus be on the wine."

"Readers identify with photographs. They feel like they know you a little, so it personalizes the experience for them. I'm not making this up. In school, I studied the psychological behavior of the buying public. There are a lot of new theories I can share with you that demonstrate—"

"No. I have to protect the girls." When Juliana looked questioningly at him, he instantly knew how odd his words must have sounded. To divert attention, he asked, "What other thoughts do you have on promotion?"

She sighed and ran her finger down a list she'd prepared. "On the weekends, you could offer wine tastings and discussions. You have enough room here for people to stay the weekend, too."

Too many strangers. "What else do you have?"

"Large conference and business meetings in the city— you could address attendees as a cultural addition to a schedule." Juliana tapped a notepad in her folder. "This just came in, but I don't have the green light yet. There is an important event for the new Children's Hospital in San Francisco soon. Their event coordinator fell ill, so a friend referred me to them. If I'm chosen, would you consider being an underwriter? Your wine would be served at the gala and you—sorry, your wine—would be featured in all the publicity."

"Sounds like I'm going to be busy." Some of her ideas were appealing. His life was safe and serene, but perversely, he missed the excitement of his former life. He'd never felt more alive than when facing death. Back then, he'd had a cause worth fighting for.

Juliana slid a typed proposal across the table. "Here's a breakdown of what we've discussed and the deposit I'll need to begin working for you."

She was direct. He liked that. "Looks fine to me. Welcome to Chateau Laurent wines." Henri clinked his glass to hers. As difficult as it was for him, it was time he began living again. He couldn't think of a woman more full of life than Juliana Cardona.

Even as he was toasting to their success, Henri wondered how much he could trust her to tell her about his past, if he could bring himself to do so.

CHAPTER 4

"*H*ave you heard back from the fundraising committee?" Juliana paused on the Howell Mountain hillside to roll up the legs of her dungarees. She loved the views from this side of the Mille Étoiles vineyard.

Caterina shaded her eyes from the sun. "That's what I wanted to talk to you about."

"Let's stop here then. It's awfully warm today." Juliana gestured to a shady tree near the edge of a block of cabernet grapes.

"Better for the grapes, but not for us," Caterina said, laughing. She hitched the bag she carried higher on her shoulder and started for the tree.

After Caterina flung out a blanket, the two friends settled in a spot near the ripening grapes with a view of the valley below. At this elevation, they were above the fog line from the bay area, which meant hot days and cool nights—superb weather for wine grapes.

Juliana reached for Caterina's bag and drew out a bottle of wine and a loaf of warm bread her mother had just removed from the oven when she'd arrived. "You have to try this wine."

"What is it?"

"I picked it up yesterday at Chateau Laurent."

"You went to Henri Laurent's home?" Caterina let out a whistle. "Is there anything I should know about?"

Laughing, Juliana inserted a corkscrew and pulled the cork. "Henri's nice, but I'm not ready, Cat." In truth, Henri Laurent unsettled her. Maybe it had been the wine, or meeting Henri's children. Or the way he'd looked at her. Regardless, she'd had a chance to clear her mind after their meeting.

"There's no one exactly like Alfonso," Caterina said with a gentle touch to her hand. "Give this man a chance. Don't wait forever, Jules."

"You should talk." Juliana checked the cork out of habit and then poured the wine into the glasses.

"You know my circumstances are different." Catrina bit her lip and glanced down.

"I know, I'm so sorry." Juliana raised her glass. "Here's to us figuring out our lives."

Juliana watched as Caterina placed her nose inside the glass and sniffed. She held it to the sky, inspecting the color, and then swirled the wine to release more of the bouquet before checking it again. Caterina was so talented, and she trusted her opinion.

Caterina sipped slowly. Raising her brow, she said, "That's a fine cabernet."

"It's not quite at the level of Mille Étoiles, but then, few wines are." Still, Juliana liked it immensely.

"So, tell me more about Henri. I saw you speaking to him at the press event. You two seemed pretty intense."

Juliana watched a hawk soaring at eye level to the mountain, hovering whenever it spied potential prey. "We had a good meeting, and I met his two children. Anne and

Beatrice—such little ladies, but they seemed lonely way out there in Calistoga. Anyway, Henri and I shared some wine and talked." She paused, shaking her head.

"What is it?"

Juliana took a sip. "Henri has such a nice way with his children. And he was clearly in love with his wife. He's probably seven or eight, or maybe ten years older than I am and has a passion for wine. But when I'm near him, I get nervous, kind of jittery. I almost didn't go to his home."

"Hmm. He's awfully good looking, too."

Juliana fanned herself. "He looks nothing like Alfonso." As soon as the words left her mouth, she blanched. She couldn't believe she'd just compared Henri to Alfonso. "Anyway, I have to figure out how to work with him. He makes me a little ill at ease."

"That's called attraction, Jules. Or lust."

"Absolutely not." Juliana sliced the air with her hand for emphasis. "I don't plan on making any mistakes."

Caterina swirled her wine again. "None of us *plan* on it," she said quietly.

"Oh Cat, I didn't mean it like that." What was wrong with her today? Juliana touched her friend's hand with empathy. Last year, Caterina had given birth to a baby girl, but she hadn't been able to tell her mother. Ava Rosetta was a formidable force, and Caterina was sure she would disown her. She faced an insurmountable problem. It seemed there was no way out; she'd been struggling to make a heart-wrenching decision. Juliana couldn't imagine what she would do in Caterina's circumstance.

"It's okay, but you should learn from my mistakes," Caterina said, blinking hard.

Juliana hugged her. "You have nothing to be ashamed of. Marisa is a beautiful little girl." Caterina was considering giving her daughter up for adoption, a decision Juliana knew was difficult for her.

"Thank you, Jules. I'm not sure what I'll decide to do." Caterina looked up at her with moist eyes. Wiping her eyes, she sniffed, and then pushed her dark wavy hair from her face. "Let's get back to you."

"There's not much else to say." Juliana unwrapped the tea towel from the bread and tore off a piece for Caterina. "Alfonso and I were kindred spirits. I don't know if I'll ever find that again. Why marry someone, like Sherri did, only to find out your husband was keeping secrets from you?" Another childhood friend was in the process of divorce proceedings.

"Not every man is like Dennis. Sherri should have gotten to know him better before they married. She was the one who rushed him." Caterina tasted the bread. "This is delicious. But really, you and Alfonso were unique. You'd known him for years."

Juliana tried to remember if Alfonso had ever made her feel the way Henri did. They'd been friends before they began dating, so it had been different, more natural. "The number one rule to being in business is don't get romantically involved with a client. It's a sure way to lose a good client."

"Speaking of clients, I have news about the gala event. The chairwoman of the new Children's Hospital fundraising committee came to dinner with her husband at the hotel." Caterina grinned. "Alma Jenkins wants you to call her after the weekend."

"Did she say anything else?"

"Not much. It seems you got a rave review from Bessie Walters, who is one of her friends. If I had to guess, I'd say you're at the top of her list. Most of the other people who put on events like that are booked months in advance."

"I'll call Mrs. Jenkins first thing on Monday morning."

"I know you're excited, but don't sound too eager. Let her make an offer first, but if she won't, start high. Say you'll consider it and then call her back in an hour. Don't agree too quickly."

"Are you sure?"

"Positive. It will make her and the committee feel like they're fortunate to have acquired your services, so they'll respect you more." Caterina grinned. "And I found out that she does speak Spanish. She's from Argentina."

"*Muchas gracias, mi amiga,*" Juliana said. She'd been born in the San Joaquin central valley in California, but her mother had insisted she study Spanish in school so she would speak her native language properly, not like the field hands that her parents were. Nina was proud of her Mexican heritage, but she desperately wanted her daughter to have the advantage of being a well-spoken American who also sounded educated in her native language. To Nina, that began with the way Juliana spoke and conducted herself.

Juliana's mother was as strict as Caterina's mother, and she hadn't been happy when Juliana had moved away from home. In her mother's culture, young women lived with their parents until they were married. But Juliana had argued that she was practically a widow since Alfonso had died. And she was older than most unmarried women.

Juliana nibbled on the bread. "Are you sure your mother doesn't want Mille Étoiles involved in the event?"

Caterina shook her head. "She's fully committed right now. This event is all yours, Jules. It will help your business. Getting into that society crowd is a real challenge."

"Thanks for passing along a great opportunity."

Caterina clinked her glass. "Good friends stick together. Good luck, and call me as soon as you know something."

Later that evening, after Juliana had stayed for supper at the main house with Caterina, Ava, Raphael, and Nina, she'd started down the mountain's narrow road in her Chevrolet. A sliver of the moon perched in the night sky, which was illuminated with a thousand stars. She cranked down her windows to let the balmy night air in.

When she reached the boarding house where she lived, she parked in back and opened the door to the screened-in porch. The wide-planked floor creaked under her footsteps. Outside the screen, crickets chirped their evening song.

"Good evening, Juliana." Mrs. Morales peered over the top of her reading glasses. "You're home late this evening. I've been waiting up for you. At your mother's, were you?"

"I had supper at Mille Étoiles." Juliana suppressed a smile. Mrs. Morales had never married. She'd turned the large home she'd inherited into a women-only boarding house, treating residents like daughters. "I brought you a loaf of Mama's bread. I'll leave it in the kitchen."

"How thoughtful of you. Wait just a moment. Something came for you today." The woman put her knitting aside and removed her glasses. Pushing herself up from her chair, she crossed to a table near the entry to the house.

"What is it?" Juliana couldn't imagine what it was. She waited, thankful for the breeze blowing through the screen. Her room was upstairs. While it was warm during the day, the evening breeze cooled her room in the evening.

"It's a letter." Mrs. Morales smiled. "Looks like you have a youthful friend."

Juliana looked down at the letter. The handwriting was childish. The address read: Miss Juliana Cardona, Napa. It was such a small village that no street address was required. Mr. Sanders, the postmaster, knew everyone.

"Thank you," Juliana said, opening the door.

"Aren't you going to open it?"

"When I get upstairs."

"You can open it down here. I wouldn't mind."

"Thank you for your thoughtfulness, Mrs. Morales, but I'm a little tired. Good night." Juliana stifled a laugh. Her landlord lived vicariously through her boarders. She had strict rules—a curfew, no men allowed upstairs, no alcohol or tobacco, and church attendance strongly encouraged. However, she made allowances for Juliana's wine, saying that as long as the wine was there in the ordinary course of her business, it was acceptable. Especially if Juliana brought an occasional bottle of cabernet sauvignon to Mrs. Morales.

Once inside her room, Juliana kicked off her espadrilles and sank onto the white chenille spread covering an iron-framed bed that squeaked when she sat down. Curious, she opened the envelope.

Dear Miss Juliana Cardona,

We liked meeting you very much. And we loved you too. You can be our mother. Because we do not have one. We want to see you soon again. We hope you do too.

Love,

Anne and Beatrice

P.S. Henri is nice too. You can get married.

· · ·

Juliana laughed, delighted with the letter the girls had clearly composed and written. She wondered how they had managed to mail it. Did Henri know? Surely not. It would be a secret between her and the girls, she decided, admiring the hearts the girls had drawn on the letter.

After washing her face and climbing into her creaky spring mattress bed, Juliana thought about Anne and Beatrice and how lonely they must be. At least she'd had friends her age at Mille Étoiles when she was a child.

She snuggled into her clothesline-fresh cotton sheets. Before she said her prayers and turned off the lamp on her nightstand, she decided that even if she were on purely professional terms with Henri, she could still be friends with the little girls.

CHAPTER 5

*J*uliana hurried from her afternoon tea meeting to a phone booth inside the lobby of the Palace Hotel in San Francisco. Sunlight streamed through the ornate arched glass ceiling behind her in the garden court. She closed the folding glass door against the din of the lobby and perched on the wooden bench, adjusting the narrow skirt of the square-necked, fitted dress she'd sewn herself. In a vivid shade of claret red, the dress matched her small felt hat, and she'd paired her ensemble with cream-colored gloves. Removing a clip-on rhinestone earring, she picked up the telephone receiver.

After the operator put her call through, Juliana clutched the phone, grinning broadly when she heard his deep voice. "I have great news for you, Henri. The Children's Hospital fundraising committee would be thrilled to serve Chateau Laurent wine at its gala next week. They loved your wine!"

"That's wonderful," Henri exclaimed. "Where are you right now?"

After she told him, he said, "Stay right there. I'm taking you to dinner."

"You're not driving to the city now, are you?"

"Why not? This calls for a celebration. We'll make it an early night if you like, but celebrate we will."

Henri sounded so excited that Juliana relented, laughing.

"Can't wait to see you, Juliana." His voice dropped a notch. "I've kind of missed you."

"It's only been a few days, Henri. And I've been working on your publicity campaign."

"You can tell me all about it when I see you. I'll kiss the girls and be on my way."

After hanging up the telephone, Juliana sat in the muffled quiet of the telephone booth for a moment, trying to sort out her feelings. Her heart was pounding, she was unreasonably excited about seeing him. She kept telling herself he was only a client.

When Henri arrived at the front of the Palace Hotel, Juliana slid into his shiny red Cadillac Eldorado convertible. Henri greeted her in the European fashion with a kiss to each cheek. Juliana struggled to maintain her composure and appear cosmopolitan, but inside her nerves were doing the cha-cha.

"What a grand time we're going to have." Henri sounded even more enthusiastic than on the telephone. "I've got a treat in store for you."

"Well, don't hold back," she said, laughing. "I hope I've dressed appropriately."

He glanced appraisingly at her and smiled. "You look sensational. We could go to a fancy Nob Hill restaurant, or we could have a culinary adventure. Which one do you vote for?"

"Adventure, any day."

Henri grinned at her. "Do you like Chinese food?"

"Absolutely," Juliana replied. After the formal tea she'd

had at The Palace, this idea sounded like fun.

"Chinatown, here we come." He turned onto Market Street and wound through Union Square to Grant Avenue.

Soon they were driving through the festive lights of Chinatown. Strings of red lanterns lined Grant Avenue and the shops shimmered with beautiful offerings. Juliana loved it, even though she knew it wasn't truly authentic. After the earthquake and fire of 1906, the area had been rebuilt in an Americanized 'Oriental' fashion. Still, if she closed her eyes and drank in the aromas and sounds, it was as if they'd flown across the sea and landed in Hong Kong or Shanghai. "Do you come here often?"

"I used to. But not that often."

"Did you and Solange come to Chinatown much?" Juliana was trying to make pleasant conversation, but she was also curious about the life they'd shared.

"We did. She liked shopping for silk fabric, incense, porcelain, and food. I have a lot of good memories here."

Henri pulled up to a restaurant. "And here we are. Hope you can use chopsticks."

Johnny Kan's restaurant was well-known for fine Cantonese-style dining, but Juliana had never been here. They were immediately shown to a table in the high-ceilinged restaurant. To Juliana's surprise, the kitchen was separated only by a glass wall. Diners could watch the master Chinese chefs at work.

"How fascinating," Juliana said, watching chefs toss vegetables into large woks, add sauces, stir a few times, and quickly turn the food onto a plate. Henri seemed like he was in his element, exploring the menu and talking to the waiter. Juliana was enjoying the stylish setting.

"This is the finest Cantonese-style restaurant in the

United States," he said. "What kind of Chinese dishes do you like?"

"Any kind of seafood. Crab, shrimp, fish. Lots of vegetables. Bird's nest soup."

"Mind if I order for you?" When she agreed, Henri began to speak to the waiter in half-English, half-Cantonese.

"You speak Chinese?"

Henri laughed. "I don't think I could be accused of that. Arrested for it, perhaps." He made a face. "Solange and I studied Chinese when she was sick. During that time, we had a chef from Canton who had also trained in Paris. The girls grew up on Chinese, French, and American fare."

Juliana thought about the sweet note they had sent. For a moment she was tempted to tell him but thought better of it. That would remain their secret. "They've been real troopers, those girls."

Henri started to say something else, but he seemed to think the better of it. Juliana rested her chin in her hand, listening to him talk about his new ideas to build his wine business.

The more Juliana learned of him, the more questions she had. It seemed as if there were another story lurking just beneath the surface of the conversation. She couldn't say why she felt that; it was more of a sense than anything he'd said. Or perhaps she was mistaken.

"How're you doing?" Henri asked, his eyes sparkling.

"Couldn't be better." And that was the truth. She was really enjoying herself.

A waiter served steaming tea while they talked. Henri transformed before her eyes from the quiet, reticent man he'd been at her press event to a man more at ease in her company. Juliana sat back, enjoying the sound of his deep melodic voice as he recounted anecdotes about Anne and Beatrice and Solange. She didn't mind that he talked about his wife, though why should that matter to her anyway? In fact, he seemed to become more relaxed as he did, so she encouraged him with questions.

As Henri recounted fond memories, her mind wandered to Alfonso, and she wondered if he would have liked this restaurant. Why that comparison bothered her, she didn't know, but it did. She sipped her tea, thinking. Maybe it was because he had been in her life for years, but now she was having new experiences without him. Did Henri feel like that, too?

After they'd finished the soup, other dishes began to arrive. Aromatic rice, delicate crab topped with garlic and scallions, vegetable crepes, savory flounder with julienned ginger. Henri was eager to share his favorites with her.

After they'd eaten all they could, Henri began to ask questions about the gala. "How many people will be in attendance?"

"About four hundred, I understand."

"What is being served for dinner?"

Juliana outlined the menu. "Could you donate some wine for the auction?"

"Of course," he replied. "And what do you plan to wear?"

"I haven't even thought of it." Although the committee *had* asked her to make some introductions and oversee the auction. "Oh my goodness, I *do* have to find a dress." She added shopping to her ever-lengthening mental list of tasks.

Henri cleared his throat. "Since we both have to attend, I'd be honored if you would be—"

"Thank you," she interjected, before he could say *date*

or whatever he might have said that would have been awkward. "I'd definitely appreciate a ride."

If Henri were disappointed, he hid it well, she noted. He only hesitated for a moment.

After leaving the restaurant, Henri wanted to walk around Chinatown. As they passed storefront windows, Juliana admired slim cheongsam dresses and brilliantly colored textiles displayed in lighted shop windows.

They strolled into a boutique that had simple necklaces and charm bracelets. A lovely scent of sandalwood incense filled the air.

A wizened woman behind the counter greeted them. She asked Juliana, "What is your birth year?"

Henri studied Juliana with interest. "Some women don't like to share their age. Are you one of those?" His vibrant, cognac-colored eyes crinkled at the corners as he smiled.

"I don't mind," she said, laughing. "I'm twenty-seven, and I was born in 1929. That's considered old-maidsville in Mexican years."

"I think it's just right," Henri said.

The woman was nodding to herself. "Year of the snake. A very good sign." She turned to Henri. "She is intelligent, brave, and charming. You are a lucky man."

Henri's face deepened in color, and Juliana realized he felt put on the spot. "Oh, no, we're not together," she said to the women. "We're only friends. Business associates."

The woman's eyes sparkled. "If you say so." She brought out a bracelet that had a few Chinese good luck charms on it that Juliana recognized. "I can put a snake charm on this for you. It will bring you much luck."

"Then we must have it," Henri said.

"Oh, no." Juliana wasn't comfortable accepting a gift from him, though it was an unusual, beautifully crafted bracelet. She'd often admired charm bracelets, but until her business became more successful, jewelry wasn't on her shopping list.

"It's my pleasure. We're celebrating our first success in the new publicity campaign tonight. I insist we commemorate it. Besides, we need to keep the good luck rolling in."

She couldn't deny his argument. "Okay, then. Thank you," she said, while the woman measured her wrist and selected a charm for her.

"What a beautiful red dress you're wearing," the woman said as she reached for her jewelry tools. While she worked, she told Juliana about her Chinese sign. "As a snake, red is your lucky color. Snakes are very intuitive. And for love, you are best suited to a rooster." The woman peered at Henri. "Are you a rooster?"

"Some people have told me I like to crow about my wines. Does that count?"

The woman shook her head. "What is your birth year?"

Teasing him, Juliana cupped her hand around her ear. "What's that, Henri? Speak up."

He tapped her nose. "If you must know, 1921. I'm eight years older than you. Satisfied?"

She was. He was thirty-five years old. About what she had guessed. Not that it mattered, of course.

"Then you are doubly blessed," the woman said, reaching for another charm. "You are a rooster. You two are well-matched." To Juliana, she said, "He is talented, hard-working, and honest. Even if he does like to boast a little," she added with a chuckle.

Grinning, Henri held up a finger. "Only about my amazing wine."

Juliana crossed her arms, sizing him up. "The talented part is certainly correct. Hardworking, check. Boastful, check. And honesty is definitely important." She couldn't abide people who weren't truthful.

"There. You try it on." The woman held out the bracelet for Juliana and clasped it around her wrist. "Perfect size for you. Great luck will soon be yours."

Henri paid for the bracelet, and they left. As they walked, Juliana said, "You didn't have to do that, you know."

"No, but it gave me pleasure. It's been a long time since I bought something for a woman. I'm a man. That makes us feel good, so humor me. I'm your client, remember? So, you have to accept my gifts."

"That's not the way it works, but I do appreciate it." The bracelet tinkled as she moved her hand. She liked the subtle reminder of the evening they'd spent together.

When they got back into Henri's Cadillac, he asked if she'd brought her car to the city.

"I did. It's parked at The Palace Hotel."

"It's late. I'll drive you home. I have an appointment with a printer here in the city tomorrow so I could drive you back in. And I could really use your help on the new wine label."

"The one Solange was working on?"

He nodded. "You were right. It is a nice tribute to her."

Juliana was pleased he'd taken her advice. "I'd enjoy that. And thank you for the ride. It is getting late. It will almost be past my curfew."

"Your *what?*" Henri turned to her with an incredulous look on his face.

Laughing, she said, "My landlady at the boarding house is pretty strict. Mrs. Morales likes to say she runs a tight ship."

"I'll say. Sounds like you're in the navy." He checked his

watch. "Better have you back on time, then. I wouldn't want to get on the bad side of Mrs. M."

"Don't worry," she replied, grinning. "Everything is copasetic, Monsieur Laurent."

Henri put the top down on his cherry red Eldorado Cadillac while Juliana removed her hat. He turned on the radio, and an Elvis Presley song was playing. In a rich, deep voice he sang out, "Love me tender..."

Juliana sang with him. They exchanged smiles and belted out the song as they whizzed across the Golden Gate Bridge with a thousand stars shimmering around them.

As Henri wound his way to Napa, he talked about wine and Juliana stole looks at him from the corner of her eye. Henri had a strong, aristocratic profile. She thought of the upcoming gala and wondered idly what he'd look like in a tuxedo. Not that it mattered, she told herself.

Rooster or not, he was only her client.

CHAPTER 6

*J*uliana stepped onto a round riser in front of a three-way mirror in the dressing room. "How about this dress?"

"I love that one," Caterina said. She sat with her white cotton gloves spread across the lap of her trim, robin's egg blue faille suit.

"It's the color of cabernet, isn't it?" Juliana twirled around, checking the back in the mirror. The dress had a trim bodice that rested slightly off the shoulders. From the waist, the satin dress curved to fit her and then flared at the hem.

Juliana had called Caterina, hoping she could join her on her lunch break from the St. Francis Hotel. She needed a second opinion on an evening dress. Though she loved beautiful clothes, she'd been brought up in dungarees in the vineyard, as were most of the children in the valley.

Turning on the riser, Juliana inspected the fit. Pale pink moiré wallpaper reflected in the mirror, casting a soft rosy glow in the fitting room and across her skin. Juliana loved shopping, though it still seemed extravagant to her. Two or three store-bought dresses or suits a year was what her budget allowed; she still sewed most of her clothes. She or her mother had made most of her best dresses when she was growing up. Juliana was more accustomed to gingham than satin.

"It's so elegant." Juliana lifted her hair from her neck and wound it into a bun, considering the effect. "And red is supposedly my lucky color. I have it on good authority."

"From whom?"

Juliana jingled her new gold bracelet. "A Chinese jeweler told me so. I'm a snake and red is lucky for me."

"A snake?" Caterina looked at her with mock suspicion. "What have you been up to?"

She told Caterina about the dinner celebration she'd had a few days ago with Henri and their visit to Chinatown. "He gave me this bracelet to mark the occasion."

"It's lovely. So unusual," Caterina said, taking a closer look at the bracelet. "Does this have a deeper meaning between you two, by chance?"

Juliana threw her a look. "Not at all. He's my client."

"If you say so." Catrine shrugged nonchalantly, but her eyes glittered with happiness.

Turning back around, Juliana stared at her image in the mirror. That was precisely what jeweler had said, but of course, there wasn't anything to it. "Rooster, indeed," she mumbled, as she slid the zipper down.

Caterina caught her eye in the mirror. "What did you just say about a rooster?"

The days flew while Juliana busied herself with the details of the gala. From food to flowers, music to seating arrangements, Juliana tended to all the final details. She contacted editors of local newspapers and magazines to invite them and pitch coverage of the gala, including the fact that the exclusive—and seldom seen—Chateau Laurent wines were to be served. Reporters from both the *Examiner* and the *Chronicle* wanted to interview Henri, too.

When the day of the gala finally arrived, Juliana dressed in her wine-colored evening gown. From Caterina, she'd borrowed ivory-colored satin gloves that rose above her elbows. Her hair was wound into an elegant chignon. She clasped the charm bracelet Henri had bought her over her gloved wrist.

After she was ready, she went downstairs to wait in the boarding house living room. Mrs. Morales was there, too, her knitting needles clicking in the quiet room. When they heard a car outside, they both looked out the window.

"Is that your young man?" Mrs. Morales patted her hair. "He's terribly handsome. Here he comes. You should go upstairs. Hurry."

"But I'm ready."

Mrs. Morales pushed her toward the stair. "Don't let him know you're waiting. A gentleman caller should wait for you to make your grand entrance."

Juliana rolled her eyes. "He's not a gentleman caller. He's my client. I'm staying right here—even if he were my date." She blew out a breath of exasperation. Thank goodness times were changing.

Still fretting, Mrs. Morales rushed to open the door at Henri's knock. "Your gentleman is here," she announced.

At that, Juliana smiled through gritted teeth. "Henri, so good of you to come. May I present Mrs. Morales, my landlord." She gestured to Henri. "Mr. Laurent, proprietor of Chateau Laurent wines and my client." She emphasized the last word, but Mrs. Morales was already gushing over

Henri. Juliana pressed a hand to her fluttering heart. He *did* look handsome in his tuxedo.

"*Con mucho gusto,*" he said.

She thought Mrs. Morales might faint when Henri lifted her hand to whisper a kiss above her skin.

Henri placed a bottle of Chateau Laurent cabernet sauvignon on the table. "I thought you might enjoy a bottle of my wine, too."

Mrs. Morales bloomed with anticipation. "*Muchas gracias.* However, I only drink a little for medicinal or religious purposes. I'll put it away."

Juliana smothered a smile. "You didn't look well this morning. Maybe you should have a glass after supper."

Mrs. Morales coughed into her hand. "Maybe I should. And Mr. Laurent, no need to worry about Miss Cardona's curfew tonight."

"Thank you, ma'am." Henri turned and exchanged an amused expression with Juliana.

As Henri helped her into the car, Juliana caught a whiff of his cologne. Lemony, wooded, and warm, it melded with his natural scent and drew her in. "Thank you," she managed to say in a calm, professional voice.

Before he closed her door, he paused. "You're an absolute vision."

"It's the dress," she said, touching the satin bodice.

"No, it isn't." His eyes were magnetized to hers. "But it is extraordinary on you."

Inside the grand ballroom at the St. Francis Hotel, Juliana was pleased with the decorations she'd arranged, which matched the splendor of the ornate room. Crystal chandeliers sparkled above round tables laden with china, crystal, and silver.

One of Juliana's housemates was a teacher in Napa, so she'd asked for her help. To help raise money for the Children's Hospital, her friend had children of all ages at the school draw cards that said *Welcome*. Some were illustrated with crayons and finger paint, while others were more advanced charcoal sketches or watercolors. Juliana hoped these would encourage guests to open their wallets even more for such a good cause.

If tonight were financially successful, the committee would meet its goal to fund the new hospital. Juliana had also asked them to consider funding children's clinics in Sonoma and Napa, too. There was a real need, especially for migrant families who picked grapes during harvest season. Committee members had been unaware of this need and promised to help.

"I had no idea you were so talented and organized," Henri said, looking impressed.

"To me, this is fun." Juliana smiled up at him. "I love bringing people together for an important cause. And helping good people like you expand their business."

Henri smoothed a wisp of hair from her forehead. "You have no idea how much I appreciate what you're doing," he said, lowering his voice.

Juliana felt her face grow warm. "The reporters who want to talk with you should be arriving any minute. I told them to come early." She glanced toward the doorway. "People are beginning to arrive. I'd better help the volunteers at the door. Thanks for helping me with the seating cards and the children's artwork."

"I enjoyed it." He kissed her on the cheek. "Go."

Juliana hurried to the front, touching her cheek where

he'd casually kissed her, her bracelet tinkling as she lifted her hand. He was probably just being polite.

A young man with a press credential tucked into his hatband appeared at the door. Juliana waved and crossed the ballroom to meet him.

She introduced herself and directed him to Henri. "But no photos of Mr. Laurent, please." When the reporter looked bewildered, she added, "He's very modest and private." As she watched Henri greet the young man, she wondered again why he was so against having his photo taken. Frankly, that had started to concern her. But she didn't want to think about that now.

Juliana took her place to greet the guests. "Good evening, Mr. and Mrs. Crocker." Several of the guests were clients, too. Thanks to Caterina's referrals, she'd helped many people design and stock their private wine cellars with the finest wines their region had to offer, from wineries such as Mille Étoiles, Charles Krug, Louis Martini, and Inglenook.

She admired the parade of fashionable evening wear. All around her, women sparkled in voluminous skirted dresses or slim, elongated styles, with jewels sparkling at their throats and wrists.

Guests began to mingle and soon the evening was underway. Juliana and Henri sat together at dinner, but she hardly touched her food. She was busy organizing the speakers. As dessert and coffee were served, Juliana stepped up to the podium to introduce the evening's speakers, including a noted pediatric doctor.

At the end of the presentation, she returned to the podium. "I'd also like to introduce the proprietor of Chateau Laurent Wines, whose wine you're enjoying this evening. Please join me in welcoming Henri Laurent."

Amid applause, Henri made his way to the front. In his rich, knee-weakening baritone, Henri spoke briefly about his passion for wine and the methods he employed to raise his cabernet wine to new levels of excellence. Then he praised the group for its commitment to children's medical care.

Juliana watched the guests as he spoke. Henri's voice mesmerized the women in the crowd, and she saw several men study the Chateau Laurent wine bottles she'd placed on each table.

When Henri stepped down from the risers that comprised the stage, she whispered, "You were so eloquent."

"They're not such tough crowd," he said with a shrug.

"They loved your wine. I heard several comments." Juliana motioned to the orchestra conductor to begin. Soon music filled the ballroom.

Several couples immediately took to the dance floor, waltzing across the room with elegance.

"Would you care to dance?"

"Would I ever," Juliana said. "I'm so relieved that's over. Now I can relax and enjoy the evening with everyone else."

Henri led her to the dance floor and took her in her arms, and then gracefully guided her to the melodic strains of the waltz.

Juliana was nearly breathless. Being in his arms was like nothing she'd ever experienced. "Where did you learn to dance like this?"

He laughed. "Boarding school, before the war. Dances were regularly organized to teach all us little hooligans how to be proper gentlemen."

"It worked," she said, smiling up at him.

"I'm rusty. I don't get much practice." His face lit with

pleasure. "I'd like to dance more often. Maybe you can accompany me."

"Maybe." Outwardly, she was poised, but inside she was a jumble of emotions.

They danced on, taking breaks only to rest or chat with a guest. Juliana couldn't remember when she'd had so much fun. Now that Henri had relaxed, he proved as good a conversationalist as he was a dancer. They laughed and talked as they swirled around the dance floor.

"Had enough, yet?" Henri had been teasing her about her bottomless supply of energy. "You young whippersnappers are apt to wear out old men like me," he said, mimicking an old man's voice.

"Hardly. You're the one who's been dragging me around the dance floor. I'm just following."

"It's about time you did that," he said with a wink.

"Hey, I've let you lead." Juliana laughed. "Most of the time, anyway."

"It's your forceful personality, but that's okay. When you lead it gives me a chance to rest."

She tapped him playfully on the chest. "You're joking with me."

Henri raised an eyebrow. "Am I?" He laughed and in a dramatic movement, dipped her low to the floor.

When he brought her back up, they were nose to nose, so close that Juliana could feel his breath on her cheek. They were motionless for a moment, caught in a trance.

"Let's sit the next one out," Henri murmured. Taking her hand, he led her from the ballroom onto an adjoining terrace where they were alone. They leaned against a low stone wall, gazing into the night sky. A harvest moon hovered over the skyline, shimmering on the bay below.

The night air was cool, and Juliana shivered involuntarily.

"Here, take my jacket." Henri shrugged out of his tuxedo jacket and draped it over her shoulders. He rubbed her arms to warm her and drew her close to him.

Juliana looked up to thank him, but his lips were so close to hers that words failed her. A moment later, their lips met cautiously.

"You have no idea how long I've wanted to kiss you," Henri whispered. Enveloping her in his arms, he deepened his kiss.

At first, Juliana responded hesitantly. His kiss was nothing like she'd ever known; his desire was that of a man, unmistakable and overwhelming. As his lips lingered on hers, his hand trailed from her neck to the small of her back, pressing her gently toward him.

With this slight movement, Juliana was drawn to him. His lips were warm, moist, and tasted of cabernet wine. Soon, her senses were fully engulfed. The sound of the orchestra faded away, the night air warmed, and they were in a world of their own making. Nothing else existed but this moment and the feel of his hands on her face, her neck, her arms. Responding to his touch, she slid her hands over his shirt, exploring his muscular chest beneath.

She didn't know how long they'd been entwined in each's others arms when he tightened his grasp. Overcome with passion, he lifted her from the ground and whirled around. Juliana laughed with joy.

"What in the name of heaven am I going to do with you?" he exclaimed, burying his face against her neck and teasing her earlobe with his tongue.

Juliana pulled him to face her, her palms pressing against his cheeks. With her eyes focused on his, she sought to catch her breath. Never had she felt so overcome with desire. Not even with Alfonso, the man she'd planned to spend the rest of her life with. "What have you done to me?"

"Me? I was fine until you insisted I attend your press event." Henri lifted her hand and kissed it.

"Which you didn't want to come to."

"Now that would've been the worst mistake of my life. I'm so glad I let Raphael coerce me into going."

Juliana touched her lips to his again. These few minutes of passion had changed everything. Her heart and common sense were warring within her, but she didn't care about anything but being in his arms.

"I have someplace I'd like to take you."

"I can't, Henri. No, I won't."

Henri looked horrified at her thought. "No, that's not at all what I have in mind. Well, maybe it is, but I'm a gentleman. I will not compromise you." When she looked hesitant, he added, "Even Mrs. Morales thinks I'm a gentleman."

Juliana laughed at the thought of her landlord. "Ah, but you bribed her with a bottle of wine."

"A *very* good bottle of wine."

"Indeed it was." Juliana couldn't hide her excitement. "So where are you taking me? Another adventure?"

"You'll see." With a mischievous smile dancing on his lips, he took her hand and led her through the ballroom.

CHAPTER 7

"*W*hat are we doing at the marina?" Juliana asked as she hitched up a pinch of her long evening dress between her forefinger and thumb.

Henri took her hand and led her along the wooden walkway past boats that bobbed in their slips. Since Solange had died, he'd spent many afternoons here while the tutor worked with the girls. This escape had been therapeutic for him at a time when he'd desperately needed it. He couldn't wait to show her one of his prize projects.

"Here she is." Henri stopped in front of a sleek wooden yacht with masts that reached toward the sky. He felt like a kid again, proudly showing off his first sailboat.

Juliana let out a whistle. "She's a beauty."

Henri climbed onto the deck and held out his hand to help Juliana. She removed her high heels and stepped aboard.

"This is a real treasure." He ran his hand along gleaming mahogany trim. "I've spent the last year having her restored."

"How old is she?"

Henri put his arm around her. "She was built in 1926 on the Scottish island of Bute. Alfred Mylne out of Glasgow designed her. She's a 56-foot sloop, and she's come a long way. I could sail around the world in this." He noticed Juliana was shivering. "Want to go below? Or I could bring blankets and pillows up."

"Bring some blankets so we can stay above and watch the stars. It's such a beautiful night."

"Then I'll be right back."

He went below and returned with cushions and woolen blankets. He spread out the cushions and then draped a blanket around Juliana's bare shoulders. After excusing himself again, he returned with a crystal snifter. "Thought you might like a nightcap," he said, handing her a balloon-shaped glass of amber-colored cognac. Trailing a finger along her face, he teased her lips with his.

"That will warm me in no time. So will the cognac." Her eyes sparkled as she inhaled the rich perfumed bouquet. "Not one for yourself?"

"I might have a sip, but I still have to drive us back to Napa. Though sometimes I stay here. Mrs. Peabody lives in, so the girls are fine with her." He leaned back on the cushions and held her next to him, searching the constellations overhead.

This was the dream that had sustained him for so many years. A fine boat, a beautiful woman by his side, a peaceful evening. He grazed her lips and sighed, finally feeling fulfilled. This was only the beginning of what he had planned for them, if she would have him.

Juliana lifted her face to his and moonlight lit her eyes. He searched her lovely face, trying to read the thoughts behind her dark gaze. "I've been looking for you all my life," he said, caressing her shoulder. "I have never met a woman like you."

As soon as he'd said that, he felt her stiffen under his touch. "You can trust me, Juliana." He relaxed his hold on her. "I respect you. I'll promise I'll wait for you as long as you wish."

"No, it's not that." Juliana sounded confused. "I—I'm concerned. You speak as if you've forgotten all about Solange." She hugged her arms around herself.

"Not at all. I will never forget her. Solange was an important part of my life and the girls' lives for many years. Of course I miss her. We were more than family; we were the best of friends." Now he was baffled. Why was Juliana so concerned about Solange?

"It's good to hear you say that," she said, but she didn't sound convinced. "She's only been gone a year."

"She'd been trying to talk me into going out and having a life before she died, but I couldn't leave her then."

"I should certainly hope not!" Juliana looked at him as if he'd lost his mind.

Henri rubbed his forehead. Why was this beautiful evening suddenly going wrong? "Look, she just wanted me to date, get married and have a normal life. What was wrong with that? We'd been through hell together. She was an amazing woman, but she's gone."

Juliana stood up, throwing off his jacket and blankets. "I don't know if this is some modern way of thinking or what, mister, but I can't believe you would have even *thought* of dating while your wife was dying. You're despicable. I knew you were too good to be true." She spun around, grabbed her shoes, and marched to the edge of the deck.

"No, no, no. Solange was *not* my wife."

Juliana jabbed her hands on her hips. "That's even *worse*. You have two children together."

Pressing his hands against his temple, Henri let out a strangled yell. "Damn it, what is going on here? Anne and Beatrice are not *our* children. They're my wards."

"You," Juliana said, pointing to him, anger flashing in her eyes. "There is something very, very wrong with you. And this entire charade. How dare you deny your wife and children to me? Everyone in the valley knew you were married. Get me out of here now."

Henri scrubbed his face in frustration. There was no getting through to her. "Fine, I'll take you home."

"No. I am not driving back with you. Take me to the St. Francis. I'll stay there tonight." Juliana stormed ahead of him to the car.

When Henri arrived, she was sitting in the front seat with her arms crossed. He flung his jacket onto the backseat and started the car. "There has clearly been a misunderstanding. Let's talk about this." How had this night gone off its tracks? His head was spinning. "Juliana?"

She said nothing, but stared straight ahead.

"Please listen. There's a lot you don't know about me." How could he even begin to tell her about his past now?

When she didn't reply, he gave up. The silence was as thick as the fog rolling into the city.

Henri arrived in front of the St. Francis Hotel, and the doorman opened her door. Juliana was out in a flash, but not before he saw tears streaming down her face.

With his heart aching, Henri watched her walk into the hotel and out of his life. Swearing, he banged his hands against the steering wheel. What the hell had just happened?

"Move along, sir," the doorman said, waving him on.

Fighting back tears of his own, Henri yanked the wheel and turned the car toward the marina. He didn't feel like driving back to Napa, not when he'd just lost the woman who meant everything to him.

CHAPTER 8

or days Juliana ignored Henri's telephone calls, despite her landlord's pleading to call the nice gentleman back. Henri Laurent was many things, but he was not that, Juliana assured her.

Juliana lay on her chenille-covered bed staring dully at the ceiling. Caterina had brought an extra set of clothes to her at the hotel and drove her home the following day after work. Her friend had listened to her rant about Henri, commiserating with her as good friends do.

Henri had misled her—surely for devious motives, she decided—and she'd lost a client because she'd crossed the professional relationship line. She had only herself to blame. Her glamorous world didn't seem so dazzling anymore, and she wished she could crawl into a cave until her bruised pride and broken heart mended.

Now, with her anger spent, Juliana blinked back tears of despair, wishing Henri had been the man she had imagined he was.

She began to feel sorry for herself. Her sweet Alfonso, the only man who would probably ever love her, had died. However, she was not alone. Many men and women had given their lives in the Second World War and the Korean War, so the country was full of women like her who were widowed or would never marry.

The radio often blared statistics of unmarried women, and it was sobering to her. Would she end up like Mrs. Morales, running a boarding house and trying to mother every young woman who passed through her doorway?

Turning on her side, Juliana punched her feather pillow with a vengeance. But was a life like her landlord's really so bad? If the alternative was a man like Henri, she'd be just fine on her own. She didn't need a man in life, thank you very much.

She huffed in disgust. It was official; she was twenty-seven and now entering old-maidsville.

That was far better than being married to a duplicitous man.

She felt sorry for Anne and Beatrice, for having a father like that. Recalling the day she'd been at Chateau Laurent, she thought he had seemed genuine around them.

But if she were honest with herself, she'd had several questions along the way. Why had he appeared so suddenly in the valley and bought one of the largest properties around, only to hide his family away behind locked gates and doors? No one locked their homes like that here. Well, hardly anyone. What was he hiding?

Restless, she turned over again and laced her fingers behind her neck, studying the ceiling. How had he acquired that strange French-American accent he had? And why had he left Boston?

He'd told her he'd gone to boarding school and then joined the war effort in Europe. Yet, he never talked about the war, his rank, or his branch. Every other man she knew who'd been in the armed forces had something to say about it. There had been nothing in his home to suggest he'd ever been at war.

Nothing.

That was suspicious in itself. No, there were too many clouds around Henri Laurent, and she didn't want to weather the storm.

Thinking about him and her lonely life ahead, Juliana's eyelids grew heavy.

Suddenly, her eyes flew open. That day at his home, hadn't Anne and Beatrice called him *Henri*? She was almost sure of it. Spying the letter the girls had written to her on her dresser, she pushed off the bed and snatched it.

There was proof at the end of the letter: *P.S. Henri is nice too.*

Who calls their parents by their first name? Maybe some precocious children did. But these were sweet girls.

Who looked nothing alike and were both eleven years old. On the boat, Henri had called them his wards, but she'd been too stubborn to listen.

Juliana sat on the edge of the bed, her head suddenly pounding. Drawing her hands over her face, she had a sinking feeling. Could there have been truth in Henri's words?

She couldn't sit still. Jumping from the bed, she paced the room, thinking. Then she jerked open her bedroom door and raced downstairs.

One of her housemates was on the phone. "Oh, for Pete's sake," Juliana cried. She made a rolling gesture with her hand for the other woman to hurry up.

Her housemate frowned, shook her head, and turned her back to her.

"What's the rush?" Mrs. Morales looked out from the

kitchen where she had been cooking. The center hallway smelled of chicken soup and cornbread.

"I've got to call Henri back right away."

"You should have done that a long time ago. The party line was busy all morning so Agatha just got her young man now. You'll have to wait. It's impolite to interrupt." She frowned and shook her wooden spoon at Juliana. "And pull yourself together. *Ai yi yi*, your hair is a mess."

Juliana hastily smoothed her hair into place. She waited for a few minutes, pacing the hallway, but her housemate seemed determined not to hand over the phone just to spite her.

Then again, Juliana had been awfully rude to her.

She ran back upstairs and shoved her feet into a pair of woven espadrilles. She ripped off her dirty shirt and wriggled into a clean one, buttoning her shirt with one hand and grabbing her purse and keys with the other.

She could probably make it to Calistoga before Agatha got off the phone.

Once Juliana was on the road, she tried to speed through the dusty back roads, but meandering livestock and slow farm tractors delayed her progress. Frustrated, she pulled up in front of Chateau Laurent.

The gate was locked. Of course.

She parked on the side of the road and ran to the gate. Grabbing the top railing, she hefted herself up and swung her legs over, dropping down the other side.

So much for the security of gates, she thought to herself, jogging to the front door.

Remembering her landlord's admonition, she pushed her hair back and tugged her shirt down. Something felt amiss. Looking down, she realized she'd buttoned her shirt wrong. It was lopsided.

"I can't win today," she muttered to herself. Turning around, she unbuttoned her shirt to fix it.

The door creaked open behind her. Clutching her shirt, she whirled around.

"Mrs. Peabody, oh, thank God it's you."

The housekeeper's eyebrows shot up nearly to her gray hairline. "What on earth are you doing here half-dressed?"

"I'm looking for Henri—Mr. Laurent."

"Like that?" Mrs. Peabody began to back away and close the door.

"No, no, please don't close the door." Fiddling with her buttons, Juliana shoved her foot in the doorway. "My buttons were all wrong because I was in a hurry. I'm trying to fix them."

The housekeeper looked doubtful, but sighed and kept the door open. "He's not here."

"Can I wait for him inside?"

"You'll be waiting a mighty long time. He took the children this morning and left. I have no idea when they're going to return."

"Tomorrow?" When the woman shook her head, Juliana added, "How many days?"

"Weeks, I'm afraid."

Bending over and bracing her hands on her knees, Juliana muttered a few choice words to herself under her breath.

"I beg your pardon?"

"Nothing, sorry." She raised up. "Where did they go?"

"Mr. Laurent said they were going south."

"Any specific place?"

The housekeeper shrugged.

Juliana pressed her palms together. "If he calls, please tell him Juliana Cardona is trying to reach him."

"I remember you, Miss Cardona."

"Will you tell him?"

At last, Mrs. Peabody smiled. "I'll be sure to, dear. I believe he was quite fond of you."

"Thank you, Mrs. Peabody, thank you. Tell him I—I'm quite fond of him, too." Juliana almost hugged her with joy. Instead, she grabbed her hand and shook it fiercely. "Thank you from the very bottom of my heart." She pressed her hands to her heart for emphasis and then turned to leave.

"Um, Miss Cardona?"

Juliana turned around. "Yes?"

"Your shirt. You might want to finish buttoning it."

Juliana looked down. She'd gotten only as far as the top two buttons.

After climbing over the gate again, Juliana got into her car, feeling dejected. She'd been too late. Resting her forehead on the steering wheel, she let tears fall onto her lap.

She wondered if she would ever see Henri again. Outside her window, she heard the dull rhythmic clomp of horse hooves. She looked up.

A farmer in denim overalls with a wagon of hay had passed her. Drawing the back of her hand across her tear-stained cheeks, she watched him. Fortunately, he turned near the end of the lane. She cranked the engine.

She passed the spot where the farmer had turned off. Down a narrow lane stood a country church with a graveyard to one side. A strange feeling struck her. Coming to a stop, she slid the gear into reverse, and then backed up. The farmer had stopped his horse on the other side of the church. She parked and got out.

Could Solange be buried here? Juliana walked to the graveyard. She tucked her hair behind her ear and peered at the headstones, stepping gingerly around the graves.

At the far corner of the small graveyard, she spotted a carved angel. Several bunches of wildflowers lay at the base. Juliana raced through the cemetery, zig-zagging around the plots.

She dropped to her knees by the angel. There were three clutches of wildflowers, clearly picked today and only slightly limp from the sun. Her gaze fell on the carved marker.

Here rests our beloved Solange-Marie Laurent.

Laurent. Her head spinning with doubt and disillusionment, Juliana sank her face into her hands and fell to one side, gasping between sobs.

She didn't know what to believe anymore.

CHAPTER 9

A hand touched her back, and Juliana yelped. Looking up, she held her hand against the sun until the outline of two men came into focus. One of them held out his hand.

"Come with me, child. There's a bed of ants nearby. They're overrunning this gravesite."

Sobbing, Juliana stumbled to her feet with the help of a young man wearing a priest's collar. The farmer she had passed was hurriedly brushing ants from her dungarees.

"Let's go inside," the priest said.

Once inside the stone church, Juliana could breathe easier. Incense tinged the air, and it was mercifully cool and dark. As her eyes adjusted to the dim light, she fumbled her way to a wooden pew.

The old farmer had removed his straw cowboy hat and knelt beside her. "You okay, Miss?"

"Not really," she said, feeling sheepish. How much worse could this day get? She ran her hands through her hair, picking out pieces of wild grass.

The priest returned with a glass of water. "Drink this." He sat next to her.

"If you think she's going to be okay, I'll go on yonder." The farmer jerked his thumb toward the door.

"We'll be fine. Bless you for the hay."

Juliana gulped the water and handed the glass to the priest. "Thank you, Father." He wore the collar, but he was casually dressed. He had sandy hair and didn't look too much older than she was.

"Would you like more water?"

Sniffing, she shook her head.

"Solange Laurent was a good woman. We all miss her."

At that, Juliana began crying again.

"There, there," the priest said, awkwardly patting her shoulder. "Are you a relative or friend?" He dug into his pants and produced a neatly folded white cotton handkerchief for her.

"Neither." She dabbed her eyes. "I'm just confused."

"Then tell me about it. Maybe I can help."

Juliana half rose to leave, but then she thought, what did she have to lose? Sitting back down, she said, "I've misjudged someone. Or maybe I haven't."

"Would you like to tell me who?"

"Solange's husband—her widower."

The priest listened thoughtfully. "And who might that be?"

"Henri Laurent. You probably know him."

The priest inclined his head and nodded slightly. "Go on."

Juliana spilled out the story, holding nothing back. "I knew he was a widower when we met, but then he had the gall to deny it. I told him exactly what I thought of him, that he was utterly despicable." She paused to take a breath. "But on the other hand…" She told him about the letter and her visit to his house.

"And then you stopped here. I see." The priest stroked his smooth chin. "I can clear up some of this for you. The rest will be up to you and Henri and the head guy upstairs." He pointed toward the ceiling.

Juliana nodded solemnly. "What do you think, Father?"

"I believe other people in this community—not only you—also thought Henri and Solange were married. Solange was ill, and Henri wasn't sociable, so they didn't mix much with the local community here. When people don't know the truth, sometimes they assume things."

"You mean—"

"They were cousins on Henri's father's side. They were never married to each other. Or to anyone else that I know of."

"Really? Oh, thank you, thank you." Juliana caught herself. For the second time today, she was gushing. She glanced down self-consciously. At least her shirt was fully buttoned.

"Henri Laurent is a good man." The priest rested his hand on her shoulder. "He and Solange survived the war in Europe under horrendous circumstances."

Hearing this sobering information, Juliana grew quiet.

The priest sighed. "Henri deserves whatever happiness he can find"

Juliana wondered what the priest meant. "He didn't tell me anything about the war."

"You must ask him, but this time, listen carefully to what he has to say. I think you will find a different man than the one you think you know."

"I will." Juliana brushed an ant from her dungarees, replaying in her mind the last conversation she and Henri had on his boat. Their emotions had run the gamut, from the heights of passion to the depths of despair. She regretted how she had spoken to him; she hadn't allowed him the opportunity to explain. "I have jumped to conclusions, haven't I?"

"So it would seem." He quirked a smile. "Have patience. Get to know each other better."

"Thanks for the advice, Father."

Juliana slid from the pew, crossed herself, and left the church. Leaving behind misunderstandings and immature behavior, too, she hoped.

As she drove home, disheartened over missing Henri, she felt an urge to return to the marina. She couldn't justify this impulse, but neither could she deny it.

Juliana turned toward San Francisco.

Henri was going south, Mrs. Peabody had said, but how? Her greatest fear was that his yacht would not be in its slip. She couldn't stand the thought of waiting weeks to see him. By then, it might be too late for them to repair their relationship.

An hour later, she was in San Francisco. She turned toward the marina, passing pastel macaron-colored Victorian homes dotting the way. Dense clouds obscured the afternoon sun, and a chilly fog snaked through the city.

After parking, Juliana stepped onto the wooden walkway, her heart hammering as she neared the end. Gaining strength, the wind blew whitecaps on the water. She shivered in her thin cotton shirt and wrapped her arms around herself.

Henri's yacht was nestled in its slip.

She slowed her step and craned her neck. There was no sign of movement. She stopped, hesitating. He might not even be there. Gingerly, she swung herself onto the deck. The hatch was closed and locked.

Behind her, a noise startled her. "Juliana."

Turning, she came face to face with Henri. He wore a navy jacket and a thick cable knit sweater with a canvas bag over one shoulder. With his cap angled over his eyes, she couldn't read his expression.

"What are you doing here?" he asked.

"I went to your home, and Mrs. Peabody said you had gone south. So I took a chance and came here."

Henri stared at her. "You never returned my calls."

"No." Juliana bowed her head slightly. She was ashamed of how she'd treated him.

He shoved his hands into his pockets and stared beyond her out to the bay. "I needed a break, so I'm taking Anne and Beatrice on a voyage."

"Are they here?" With her lips numbing from the cold, her words sounded strange.

"They're down below. We were leaving today, but the weather turned bad. Maybe tomorrow."

Juliana's heart was shattering. Gone was the sparkle in Henri's eyes. As quickly as his enthusiasm for life had been restored, it was once again deadened. And she'd done this to him out of her fear and ignorance.

He swung back toward her. "I'm not the monster you think I am, Juliana."

The rich timbre of his voice reverberated through her soul. She ached to feel his arms around her again. But he made no move toward her.

It was up to her.

"I know that now."

"Do you?"

"I stopped by the cemetery where Solange is buried and spoke to the priest."

"You don't trust me." Pursing his lips, Henri drew a

sharp breath through his nose. "Better we know that now than later. Good-bye, Juliana." He started toward the hatch.

"Henri, I was wrong." Shivering, she blinked back hot tears.

He stopped with his back to her.

"Wrong to accuse you of lying to me when I had based my beliefs on hearsay."

Henri turned slowly. "And I would be lying if I didn't say your actions shocked me."

Clasping her icy hands together, she said, "When Alfonso died, I was so broken that I feared risking my heart again. I didn't think I could survive another heartbreak. So I never took a chance, until you came along. Yet I don't regret it."

"Go on." Henri took a step toward her.

"I reacted the way I did out of fear. I was protecting my heart." Her teeth chattering, she added, "I might be outspoken, but I'm not normally a fire-breathing, she-devil shrew."

Wordlessly, Henri slipped off his jacket and wrapped it around her. Tilting her chin up, he met her quivering lips with his.

CHAPTER 10

*W*ith his breath forming misty clouds in the brisk air, Henri took Juliana's hand and led her down the ladder below deck. Had the weather not been bad, he'd have set sail today, perhaps never to see Juliana again. He'd even thought of selling Chateau Laurent and returning to Europe to acquire a vineyard. There he could create a new life for his small family.

But now, Juliana was back. He thought he might break down with relief. After lifting her slender frame from the ladder, he enveloped her in his arms. "I've not been honest with you, Juliana. There's so much I need to tell you."

"This time, I promise I'll listen. And I won't judge you."

"When you didn't return my calls, I thought I'd lost you forever." This was the first time since he'd returned from Europe that he'd let his guard down. Her actions had devastated him.

"I acted so foolishly." Juliana shook her head. "And ruined the lovely night we were having."

Flicking a tear from her cheek, he said, "Will you promise me another dance?"

"As many as you want."

He hoped she would still feel that way after she heard his story.

Footsteps sounded in the passageway behind them. Anne appeared in his oversized sweater. He'd put his warm clothes on the girls before he left. "Henri, did you get my clothes—Juliana!" Anne ran, her dark hair streaming behind her, and flew into Juliana's open arms.

"I knew you'd come back," Anne cried.

Beatrice raced into the galley and flung her arms around Juliana, too. "Did you get our letter?"

Juliana laughed. "I did. I thought it was so sweet of you to write."

"What letter?" Henri hadn't heard anything about this.

Anne pushed up her falling sleeves. "We sent her a letter. But it's a secret."

"If you tell him, it's not a secret anymore," Beatrice said.

"I'm not going to tell him what we wrote." Anne smiled up at Juliana. "I wrote most of it."

Henri chuckled. The girls were always up to something. "I've got your warm clothes and hot food. Which do you want first?" He opened the canvas bag he'd brought on board from the car.

"We're starving," Beatrice said, bouncing up and down.

"I take it the girls are wearing your sweaters," Juliana said. "I'll help them change if you want to put supper out."

"Thanks for helping. I hope you're staying to eat." Henri handed her sweaters and socks for the girls, and then he kissed her on the cheek.

"I think I can fit it into my schedule," she said, smiling. He'd missed that smile.

"Come on," Anne said. "We'll show you our bedroom."

Beatrice grinned. "That's called a stateroom on a boat.

And do you know what the bathroom is called?" She started giggling.

Knocking Beatrice on the noggin, Anne yelled out, "It's the head."

Henri watched the girls take Juliana by the hand and disappear through the passageway. Was it too much to hope for that they might form a family someday? When Solange was alive, they'd been a kind of family, but after she'd died, Anne and Beatrice had been deeply affected.

Reaching into the bag, he brought out peaches, plums, grapes, tomatoes, and lettuce grown on their land, along with several types of cheese and nuts. He'd also bought hot sourdough bread and a large jar of seafood cioppino from the Tadich Grill.

After arranging the food on the galley table, he called the girls. They came racing through the passageway, followed by Juliana, who now wore one of his sweaters. He liked the way she looked in it, though it was far too large for her.

Anne and Beatrice slid into the built-in booth on one side, leaving Henri and Juliana on the other. Their eyes darting between Henri and Juliana, the two girls giggled and whispered to each other.

"Remember what I said about telling secrets in front of others?" Henri gave them a false frown, but he meant it. Still, he was relieved they'd taken to Juliana so quickly. He'd been concerned they might not like her because they'd feel she was taking the place of Solange, who for all intents and purposes, had been the only mother they'd ever known.

He and Solange had been honest with the girls from the time they could talk. They'd told them they were not their parents, but they loved them just as if they were. Henri and Solange didn't know how long they'd be able to keep Anne

and Beatrice, so they didn't want to confuse them. But as
the years went on, he and Solange had become the parents
the girls had never known.

As the boat rocked against the wind, the four of them
sat eating and laughing. Juliana seemed at ease with Beatrice and Anne. Henri made jokes with them, though inside,
he was still guarded. Would Juliana look at him differently
after she heard his story?

As the wind whistled above them, Henri took Juliana's
hand in his. "It's getting late, and the weather is bad. I'd feel
much better if you stayed here. There's another stateroom
you'll be comfortable in."

"I'd like that. We can continue our conversation, too."

After supper, Henri brought out a board game, and they
all played Monopoly. Beatrice amassed a small fortune, but
at the end she insisted on sharing her winnings with Juliana.

"Then I owe you a bedtime story," Juliana said.

At that, Anne and Beatrice rushed to bed. The girls
cuddled on each side of Juliana, mesmerized as she told
them a story that her mother had told her as a child. Rain
began to dribble onto the portholes. The girls hugged their
knees to their chest. This scene of domestic tranquility
tugged at Henri's heart. He saw Juliana fitting into their
lives, but could they offer enough to her?

After he'd tucked in the girls and kissed them goodnight, Henri put his arm around Juliana while they made
their way through the passageway. "I happen to have a
fairly decent cabernet on board. Care to join me for a
glass?"

"Only if it's your wine."

"It's my best vintage."

While the rain intensified, Henri opened the wine. He
carried the wine and two glasses to a seating area, where they

sat on a built-in couch surrounded by pillows. Finding two candles in a cabinet, he brought them out and touched a match to them. The flames flickered against their wine glasses and threw shadows on the bulkheads surrounding them. Here they were safe, protected from the elements—and the past.

Juliana raised her eyes over the rim of her glass. "Will you leave tomorrow?"

He was quiet for a moment, thinking about what he had planned. Monterey, the central coast, Marina del Rey, Newport Beach, San Diego, Baja California. Yet nothing seemed as important as the woman sitting beside him now. "We'd planned on it, but now, it depends. Or we could have a short voyage. Would you like to join us?"

"Maybe," she replied, a smile touching her lips again.

Henri touched his glass to hers. "Here's to us, and to *veritas*."

"To us and to truth." Juliana sipped her wine. She waited for him to speak.

He cleared his throat and hoped she'd understand. "My grandfather immigrated to this country from France. My father was born here and joined the United States diplomatic service, so we had moved a lot. In 1935, I was 15 years old, and they decided it would be better for me to go to boarding school to have the benefit of staying in one place."

"That's when you went to Switzerland."

"Yes, and when I finished school, my parents wanted me to return to the States. But I was young and idealistic. I had cousins in France—Solange and others—and a lot of my closest pals from school were from France. When we graduated in '38, I went for a holiday to my grandfather's vineyard."

Henri swirled his wine, staring into the shimmering depths as if gazing into a portal to the past. "Then the political borders began to shift. Hitler annexed Austria in 1938 and then took Czechoslovakia. Just a year later, the Nazis invaded Poland from the west, while the Soviets seized the eastern portion. That's when France and Britain declared war against the Nazis."

"Why didn't you come back to the States?"

"There, I was needed. I wanted to make a difference and stand up against violence and oppression. My family and friends needed me. That was so much more important to me than going home."

Henri watched the rain sluicing across the portholes, remembering just such a night long ago, hidden in the dark cellar of a farmer's home. Sweating and praying he wouldn't be discovered. Henri shuddered involuntarily.

Composing himself, he continued. "One of our friends from school—Solange's boyfriend—was forced from his home with his family. They were imprisoned in a Nazi concentration camp." He sipped his wine, trying to calm and order his thoughts. "No one ever heard from the family again. That's why Solange and I joined the resistance movement and went underground."

Juliana cradled her glass in her hands. "So you did serve in the war."

"We did what we could, all over France. I helped liberate Paris, too." As Henri stared into the candles, visions of the past took shape. The flames dredged up the memory of his great aunt's torturous death.

"Tell me what you're thinking right now," Juliana said gently.

"I can't," he said, his words strangled. For years, his

nights had been haunted by the waking nightmares he'd witnessed. He squeezed his eyes shut.

Juliana rubbed a hand along his shoulder. Henri brought her hand to his lips and kissed it. Only Solange had shared his darkest memories. When he had awakened screaming in the night, it was she who had raced to him, comforting him until he had regained control, even on some of her sickest days. She was the only one he had trusted with his secrets.

Solange was gone, but Juliana was here with him now. And it was time he tried to trust someone again, rather than locking away his heart and family. He licked his lips and began. "I was thinking about my great aunt Geraldine, one of the sweetest souls I've ever known. She died in the village of Oradour-sur-Glane in the summer of '44."

Drawing an unsteady breath, Henri went on. "Oradour-sur-Glane was a peaceful village in the Vichy-governed part of France. Acting on a tip that later proved false, Nazi SS troops stormed the village." He choked back a sob. "When I heard what happened, I went looking for her. What I found was gruesome. There, after hearing the rain of gunfire that had killed their husbands, fathers, brothers, and sons, the women and children were herded into a church."

His voice faltered, but he drew a breath and went on. "Then, the church was set aflame in what became a fiery inferno of death. The entire village was massacred. More than six hundred innocent people. I searched through… until I found my aunt's remains and then I buried her." The stench of charred bodies was forever burned in his brain. Henri wiped cold sweat from his brow and gulped his wine.

Glancing at Juliana, he could tell she was shaken. Yet

she leaned in and brought her arms around him, as if to shield his present from his past.

Henri clasped her to him. She'd pried open a rusted door in his soul where his nightmares resided. Only the sunshine of another soul could banish the darkness from this hellish dungeon. For years he'd been unable to feel pleasure. Only Anne and Beatrice could shine light into the recesses, but they were children, and he could not share what he'd been through with them.

"I'm here for you, Henri, and I'm not going anywhere. You can tell me anything. I won't judge you."

For the first time since Solange had held him on his darkest nights, he let sadness seep from his eyes. When he was spent, Juliana kissed the wetness from his cheeks. Her heart beat against his and for the first time in his adult life, he felt the depth of a woman's true love.

But there was more he needed to tell her.

He brought his hands to her face, framing the most beautiful, empathetic eyes he'd ever hoped to see. "You must know that I am not without sin. I did… things that had to be done to protect others, but I will always regret taking another life, even those of my enemies. They, too, had families and loved ones."

Juliana held him as he continued talking. He was beginning to feel as if he could tell her anything.

"Most of my work for the French resistance was disruptive. We made it hard for the Nazis to operate and advance. We jammed communications, sabotaged railroads, and blew up bridges. Solange worked with us, too. We also ferried people to the south when we could, passing them off to others who helped them escape through the Pyrenees to Spain. A lot of these escapees were downed Allied pilots who needed to return to the fight. Others were regular citizens who faced certain death if they remained—Poles, Jews, political dissidents… and so many others."

Henri poured more wine into their glasses. "One time, my team got word that a train loaded with Nazi troops and supplies was heading our way in route to Normandy. We worked out a plan to mine a train tunnel through a mountain with explosives to block the entrance before the train entered. But our equipment jammed and the connection was delayed. When it finally worked, it was a few seconds too late, and the entire tunnel caved in. Those poor souls never had a chance." He hung his head. "We saved troops at Normandy, but that day still haunts me. Most of those troops at that mountain didn't want to be there any more than we did. They were sons and brothers and husbands, too. Some blokes even had cousins in Germany—families were divided by borders. At any other time, we probably would have been friends. But wars are started by angry old men, and there was nothing any of us could do except follow orders."

He took another swallow of wine. "Now you know."

Juliana raised her eyes to his. "You were at war."

"On the other hand, we helped bring an end to the war. Did you know the Great War almost ended on Christmas in 1914 when men on both sides laid down their arms and sang *Silent Night* together and exchanged greetings and souvenirs? During the Christmas truce, French, British, and Germans came together on the Western front. They played football, swapped prisoners, and sang carols. But the commanders weren't having it, so the war dragged on. Just shows that reasonable people can usually solve their differences because we're more alike than different." He gave Juliana a wry smile. "I just wish we could have saved more people. We would have, too, if…."

"If what?"

Henri blew out a breath. "If we hadn't been captured. Me, my team. And Solange."

Juliana looked up at him, her eyes wide with shock. "What?"

"Solange was sent to the women's camp at Ravensbrück. It was rough on her. She was near death when the camp was liberated. She never really recovered."

"And you?" Juliana asked gently.

"Late in '43 I was sent to Natzweiler-Struthof in the province of Alsace, which is in northern France, but the Nazis had taken the region. We were called the *Nacht und Nebel* prisoners, meaning that we were sent there to disappear into the fog and night. Few people even knew of the camp's existence. It's where resistance fighters were sent. We were separated from the rest of the prison camp population. I managed to escape, along with a couple of others, a few months later."

Henri fell silent, though there was more, much more. He stretched his neck, trying to relieve his tension.

"I am so sorry you had to go through that." As if to soothe his troubled heart, Juliana stroked his chest. "How are you now?"

"My nightmares have decreased, but I'm told they might never go away entirely." He sighed. He had returned a changed man. Hypervigilant, reclusive, depressed. Only Anne and Beatrice could lift his spirits. When he met Juliana, she had drawn him into her sunshine, where he felt more like his happier, younger self.

Juliana was quiet for a few moments. "How did you come to have Anne and Beatrice?"

"My most cherished souvenirs," Henri said. "After the camps were liberated, I set out to find Solange. Our grandfathers were brothers, which makes us second cousins. She was like the kid sister I'd never had. Anyway, prisoners from the concentration camps poured into the DP camps for displaced persons. I visited several before I found her."

He blinked hard, remembering all they'd gone through. "Solange had a friend who had been impregnated by a guard, but unfortunately, the woman died giving birth. She had no family left, so Solange took care of the baby." He smiled. "That was Anne. Just look at that sweet child now." He paused, his eyes misting with memories.

"And Beatrice?"

"A few days later, Solange woke to little Anne's cries. When she looked in the basket, there was another infant that someone had left. So Solange claimed them both as her own." He looked down. "After the medical experiments that had been inflicted on her in the camp, she knew she'd never have children of her own. I took them all back to her grandfather's vineyard. But Solange needed more medical care. After the war, the hospitals were overcrowded and underfunded, so I brought her to my parent's home in Boston."

"That explains a lot. Do Anne and Beatrice know about their history?"

"We shared a lot with them because we didn't know if we could keep them. In the end, I claimed them as my wards in a French court to get them into the U.S. Once we arrived, we heard so much about the California wine country that we moved here. We wanted to be as far away from our wartime memories as we could get. Solange had lost her family in the war, and her grandfather left the winery to a grandson when he died. I'm glad we came here because Solange died in a beautiful, peaceful place."

"And how did you learn the winemaking craft?"

"From Solange and her grandfather. Of course, I couldn't manage Chateau Laurent without help. And that includes you, too, I hope." But to what degree? Under a professional relationship, or something more?

They both fell silent. Even if his past was too much for her to understand, he felt stronger having finally unburdened some of his heart's troubles.

"That's quite a story," Juliana finally said, her voice subdued. "I can't imagine what you went through or how you made it out alive. It makes my childish behavior seem even worse."

Outside, the rain subsided and the winds calmed. Henri caressed Juliana's face, touching his lips to her smooth skin. "So now you know my past and why I've kept to myself. And then there are the girls. I won't blame you if you decide it's too much to handle."

Henri held his breath, waiting for her reply. He knew that for the rest of his life he would bear the scars of war, but having someone who understood would make it tolerable. If she would have him.

Slowly, Juliana sipped her wine, and then pushed it aside. "Thank you for being honest with me. It's one of the most important traits I look for in people. I'm sure you feel like you took a risk in telling me about your past."

"It's a risk I had to take." He brought her hand to his lips and kissed it, keeping it close to his heart.

Juliana began to say something, but then seemed to think the better of it. Henri knew the words he longed to hear from her, but he wouldn't force them from her. Each time he saw her, his feelings only grew stronger. But he had learned to be a patient man.

CHAPTER 11

*J*uliana folded her arms under her head and stretched her woolen-encased toes toward the end of the bed, thinking about the difficulties and tragedies that Henri—and poor Solange—had lived through. The stateroom walls were thin, and as she lay awake, she could hear Henri's low, heavy breathing—almost in rhythm with the waves that slapped the wooden hull and the rain that pelted the deck above, lulling her to dreamland.

She breathed in. The musky air held the salty scent of the sea—so different from the earthy wines she often analyzed, yet just as nuanced in its own way. The night air was cool, but Henri's plaid flannel shirt and socks kept her warm.

Henri had insisted she stay the night. "The storm should pass by morning."

"Then I'll be on my way."

"Wouldn't want to worry Mrs. M.," Henri had said, kissing her.

Soft murmurs floated down the hallway. She could hear Beatrice and Anne whispering and giggling.

Juliana's eyelids felt heavy. As she rested her eyes, Henri's words floated through her mind.

"Come sail with us tomorrow," he had said, his eyes sparkling in the candlelight.

"I can't just leave," she had said, laughing. "Besides, I haven't a thing with me."

"I'll make sure you have everything you need. The girls will be disappointed if you don't come along."

"Now that's not fair," she had replied.

"Wait until morning to decide."

She had promised she would. Now, as the vessel rocked and sleep began to overtake her, she drifted to sleep.

"No, no...*no!*"

Juliana bolted upright, clasping throat, her heart thundering in her ears. It took a moment for her to remember where she was.

Henri was bellowing in his stateroom. "It's too dangerous. Get them out of there!"

Footsteps padded swiftly past her door.

Juliana's pulse raced. The desperation in Henri's cries was almost palpable.

"Stop, stop, you're going to kill them all!"

Juliana scrambled from bed, adrenaline coursing through her. She hurried toward Henri's stateroom.

Two soft voices broke through his distress. "Shh, Henri, shh, it's okay. You're having a nightmare."

Juliana rushed in. "Is he all right?" Juliana asked, alarmed.

Anne looked up, frowning. She and Beatrice were on the bed, kneeling on either side of Henri, rubbing his forehead and whispering to him. "He'll be okay," Anne said as if to convince herself.

"Get them out *now!*" Henri thrashed in bed, thrusting

his arms against an imaginary assailant. The girls recoiled in fear.

Juliana took charge and shook him by his bare shoulders. "Henri, wake up," she said in a gentle, yet firm manner. "You're safe." While the girls watched with concern, she kept repeating these words until he opened his eyes.

"Wha-at?"

"You're safe now. You just had a bad dream." She helped him sit up and brushed his hair from his damp forehead. Even though the night was cool, sweat beaded his brow and gathered on his chest.

"Juliana?" Breathing hard, Henri blinked several times and then wrapped his arms around her. "Thank goodness you're here."

"You sure know how to draw a crowd," Juliana said, managing a smile. As she held him in her arms, she wasn't sure which of them was shaking more. The muscles across his broad back were taut.

"I'm so sorry I woke you all." Henri stretched out an arm to the girls, and they snuggled next to him.

Teary-eyed, Beatrice looked up to Henri. "We're awfully glad you woke up."

Juliana realized Henri wasn't the only one in the household affected by the stress of the war, and it tore at her heart that the fallout of war burdened such young, innocent girls. Moonlight shone through a porthole, resting on the worried faces of Anne and Beatrice. They looked immensely relieved that Juliana was there. Juliana kissed Henri on the cheek, and then took Anne's soft little hand. "Let's go back to bed, girls." Glancing back at Henri, she added, "You rest, and I'll be back in a moment."

After the girls climbed back into their bunks, Juliana

tucked the covers tightly around them and kissed them goodnight. Their sweet smiles tugged at her heart.

Anne yawned and said, "Thank you for helping Henri. We always stay with him when he screams, like Solange used to do."

Juliana gathered the blanket to Anne's chin. "That's a big job for little girls. But I know you made him feel a lot better by being there." Anne's eyes fluttered, and while Juliana stroked the little girl's hair, her eyes closed.

Juliana eased herself from the bed.

Henri stood behind her, watching. He wore a robe over his pajama bottoms and held one out for her, draping it over her shoulders. They left the room as quietly as they could, the polished wooden floorboards creaking beneath their footsteps.

"Now you've seen my nightmares for yourself."

"Lots of people have suffered from combat exhaustion. It's nothing to be ashamed of." Her fiancé, Alfonso, had talked of battle fatigue among the troops. When he'd returned home on leave, she'd seen the stress he'd been under. The war had changed him, too. He'd confided in her, telling her of feeling blue and having a hard time sleeping.

Henri paused at the entry to her stateroom. "Thank you for being here." Cradling her face in his hands, he kissed her lightly on the lips.

Juliana had just regained control from his nocturnal outburst when the touch of his lips sent her heart racing again. She sank into his kiss, gliding her hands around his neck, sharing the desire that she felt surge through him.

Not since Alfonso had she felt the wondrous warmth that spread through her now. She'd never thought she'd experience this sensation of pure love again. Henri was different; he was more mature than Alfonso, but the two men shared an honesty that Juliana admired.

Despite his desire, Henri pulled away from her to maintain decorum. "Good night again, sweet Juliana."

The gleaming yacht arched through the waves, rising and falling with the motion of the morning sea. Juliana tented her hand against the morning sun, watching Henri maneuver through the sloop, the full sails resplendent against golden rays.

Last night when she had arrived at the marina, sailing the California coast to Monterey peninsula the next morning had been the farthest thing from her mind, but now, as she faced the cool breeze, she was glad. Otherwise, she would have missed all this—and him. Thinking about Henri, a feeling of love bloomed in her again.

As if reading her mind, Henri glanced at her, a smile crinkling his eyes and lighting his face. This morning he seemed as unburdened as she'd ever seen him, as though the confessions of last night had partly cleared his mind.

"Hey, beautiful," Henri called out.

Juliana smiled at him. Against his ivory, cable-knit fisherman's sweater his cheeks shone ruddy in the sun, the brilliant blue sky framing him like a photo. He looked healthy and carefree; even his voice sounded lighter than it had before. Still, she knew he harbored deep psychological damages—she'd seen her share of young men who'd return to the valley shattered by war.

Would she be up to the task of helping him heal from tragedies he'd witnessed? She had loved Alfonso to the depths of her being, and she didn't know if she could ever let her heart become so entwined ever again. When he died, the pain of loss had been so great that she had nearly succumbed to it. Only her mother and Caterina had helped her keep her sanity.

And there were the girls to consider—they needed a mother, a woman who had experience caring for children.

As attractive as Henri Laurent was, he was a complicated man.

A few hours later, Half Moon Bay came into view. After sailing around Pillar Point, they motored into the marina.

"Who's hungry?" Henri called out as he finished tying off the boat. "I know a great spot for hot clam chowder and sourdough bread."

Anne and Beatrice clambered onto the dock ahead of them.

"Hope it's casual." Today, Juliana wore another one of Henri's shirts over the dungarees she'd worn the day before. She'd knotted the shirttails at her waist.

"You look fine. I'm starting to like you in my clothes. But after we eat, I'd like to take you shopping."

They found the café in the harbor and went in. As they sat down at a table with a view of the harbor and bay, a waitress leaned in and said to Juliana, "What a lovely family you have, dear."

Juliana felt her face flush. "Oh, no, we're not—"

"Thank you," Henri said, beaming with pride. He winked at Juliana. "See, we belong together," he said, kissing her.

Beatrice and Anne giggled at this, watching every movement between her and Henri.

After they ordered, Henri pulled a folded map from his shirt pocket. "Here's where we are," he said, tapping the image. "Half Moon Bay. We can spend the day here, doing some shopping, have dinner, and then set off for Monterey in the morning." He looked across the table at the girls. "We'll visit some shops after lunch. As good as Juliana looks in my shirts, she needs a few other things to wear, don't you think?"

Juliana poked him in the ribs, laughing. She had to admit, she liked this playful side of him.

"Can we shop, too?" Beatrice seemed more interested than Anne, who was watching two men repairing fishing nets on the dock.

"Of course," Juliana said. "I'd love to treat you each to a new dress. I saw some cute sundresses in a window as we were walking. I think they were just your size."

After lunch, the four of them shopped, and Juliana bought new dresses for Anne and Beatrice. At an outdoor gear shop, Henri insisted on outfitting Juliana with all the gear she'd need for the boat, from the proper shoes to shirts, sweaters, and jackets she could layer when the cool wind kicked up on the sea.

They visited another boutique with lovely, full-skirted sundresses that nipped in at the waist and revealed her toned shoulders.

"Try this one on," Henri said, admiring a crisp white cotton sundress on a hanger. "And this one," he added, pulling out a sunny lemon-yellow dress, followed by a rosy pink shift.

"I don't need that many," Juliana said, laughing.

Henri smiled. "That's not the point, sweetheart. There's very little we really need." He handed several dresses to a saleswoman. "She'll try these on."

Juliana selected a couple of other dresses and shorts. She slipped into the dressing room to try them on. When she emerged, she twirled in front of the mirror, the full yellow skirt flaring around her legs. Behind her, the girls and Henri were grinning, and their smiles touched her heart.

Beatrice ran to her and hugged her. "You look so pretty."

Henri quirked his mouth. "I don't know… I'll kind of miss seeing you in my clothes."

"Well, I'm awfully fond of your shirt, too."

"It's yours." He grinned at her. "In fact, everything I have is yours for the taking."

Juliana felt a blush work itself from her chest to her face, and she angled her head as she hugged Beatrice to her. She had to admit, she was extremely attracted to him. But could she really help him with his trauma and the recovery he needed?

That evening, as they enjoyed fresh, seared albacore tuna from the bay, the sun sent streaming scarlet rays across the water.

Henri nodded toward the flaming sky. "Red sky at night, sailors delight."

"What does that mean?" Juliana asked.

"It's based on atmospheric systems. A red sky indicates a stable, high-pressure system moving from west to east, which means we'll have good weather tomorrow." With his eyes twinkling, he clasped her hand. "Good weather for sailing all the way to Baja California."

"I don't know, the harvest is coming soon. I promised Caterina and Ava that I would help them at Mille Étoiles." Juliana laughed. "Besides, a journey to Mexico is quite a commitment."

"Hmm, so it is." Henri slid his gaze toward Anne and Beatrice. "What do you think, girls? Are we ready for that kind of commitment?"

Grinning, the two girls nodded vigorously.

After paying the bill, they all strolled back to the yacht, carrying their shopping packages and supplies. Juliana couldn't remember the last time she'd had such a nice day.

She took turns with Henri reading a bedtime story to the two girls, and soon the girls were fast asleep, exhausted after such excitement.

Climbing the ladder to the deck above, Juliana looked up. A cascade of stars blanketed the night sky like so many fairy lights. Tonight was balmy, and she'd draped a light sweater over her sundress. Behind her, with a wine bottle tucked under his arm and two glasses in his hand, Henri hoisted himself up the ladder above deck. They settled on a low bench covered with blue sailcloth cushions. Juliana breathed in, enjoying the fresh scent of the ocean.

As Henri eased the cork from the bottle, Juliana surreptitiously admired his lean, muscular physique, and then she dropped her gaze to the vintage. "That was a good year."

"It was, but I think this year will be even better."

She curled her legs under her, spreading the fabric of her new yellow sundress around her. "Yet you were leaving right before harvest?"

He paused and raised his eyes. "Without you in my life, the harvest didn't seem to matter much anymore. I have a foreman to see it anyway."

"What *does* matter to you, Henri? What do you want from life?"

Henri poured two glasses of wine. Handing her a glass, he said, "As you know, I have a responsibility to Anne and Beatrice. I love them as if they were my own daughters, and they are my family. They deserve the best I can give them. Beyond that, the vineyard is my profession and my passion. I've also made commitments to some of my workers who came from Europe—other survivors—and I am honor-bound to them."

He lifted his glass toward the heavens. "I could have died in prison, as many did. So I want to enjoy this second chance at life more than ever. I want to sail, hike, travel, live…" He turned to her and touched her glass. "And love."

As she listened, it dawned on Juliana that she was beginning to love everything about this deeply honorable man. Still, questions lingered in her mind, and she couldn't bear to have her heart destroyed again. "So, just what does that mean, Henri?" she asked softly. "Are you looking only for a mother for the girls?"

"I don't think they need one," he replied, tapping his glass.

Juliana felt as though her breath had been knocked from her lungs.

A slow smile spread across his face. "But we all *want* you —me, most of all. I love you, Juliana." Henri swept her into his arms.

Relief flooded her. "Oh, Henri… my love." Before she could say another word, he kissed her.

Long suppressed passion flared in her again, and a warm glow of happiness suffused her.

A few moments later, they heard giggles behind them. Anne and Beatrice were on the ladder, peering out from the galley below.

Laughing, Henri pulled back. "Better get used to this." As he started to get up, the girls burst with laughter and scrambled back down the ladder, pounding their way back to their stateroom. He gave a dramatic sigh. "That's what you have to look forward to."

"They're just excited." Juliana smoothed her dress, chuckling.

"Are you sure you're up for all this? Two active girls, a busy household and vineyard, and a broken-down man haunted with nightmares?"

"First of all, I adore the girls," Juliana said, ticking off her fingers. "Second, I grew up at Mille Étoiles, so I'm used to the craziness of vineyard life. And third, I certainly don't see a broken-down man when I look at you."

Taking her hand, he said, "I've been honest with you. These nightmares, they're a horrible part of my life. It was tough on Solange. You need to understand this."

"I do understand. More than you realize." She sipped her wine, thinking. Many of the young men in the valley that returned from the war had similar issues. Battle fatigue or shell shock, they called it. "Have you ever sought help?"

"Juliana, so many others are much worse off than I am."

"But that doesn't mean you have to live this way."

He gazed at her with interest. "What would you suggest?"

She clasped Henri's hand. "There's a good doctor in Sonoma who has helped a lot people. She uses something called talk therapy."

Henri arched an eyebrow but seemed to consider her words. "If you think it might help."

"I do. She helped one of Al's closest friends. He was so shell-shocked he could hardly sleep. But he's so much better now. I really think she could help you."

Henri gave her a light kiss. "If you have faith in this doctor, then I'll make an appointment."

CHAPTER 12

*O*ver the next two weeks, Juliana had spent every free moment with Henri, though she had yet to tell her mother or friends—not even Caterina. She wanted to savor this magical time between them.

"That's where I'd like to plant more cabernet vines," Henri said.

Hooking her arm through his, Juliana shaded her eyes and followed Henri's line of sight along a rolling hill. She walked through the well-tended vineyard with Henri, who was taking her on a more extensive tour of Chateau Laurent than before to see the entire house, vineyard, and wine-making operation.

The sun was warm on her shoulders, and she'd swept her hair back with a coral-colored scarf. She wore the white cotton sundress that Henri had bought her on their sailing trip. After stopping in Half Moon Bay, they'd sailed on to Monterey and back to San Francisco on the vintage yacht, agreeing that after harvest, they'd take an extended trip to Baja California. As her gold bracelet jingled on her wrist, the snake and rooster swung side by side. Henri wore a white T-shirt under a blue denim work shirt and jeans. On board the boat, she'd encouraged him to relax and adopt a more casual style.

They'd all had fun in Monterey. Beatrice and Anne were amazed at the otters and seals frolicking in the bay, and at low tide they spotted an assortment of sea creatures they'd never seen before. The four of them had sailed around the Monterey Peninsula admiring the breathtaking scenery, where windblown cypress trees lined the shores. Juliana had never seen Monterey from the ocean vantage point, and it was utterly spectacular.

Henri brushed a few wisps of hair from her forehead. "After our trip, I feel reinvigorated. Being on the water, breathing in the fresh sea air, and most of all, being with you, gave me a chance to look at life through a new lens, to imagine what the future might hold for us."

"I agree," Juliana said. "I feel I've been given a second chance to build the life I've always dreamed of."

"Both of us. I want to create a new life together." Henri paused. "I've been places where a morsel of food, a blanket, or a small show of mercy meant the difference between life and death. Though I will never forget, now I've been given an opportunity for a life few can ever hope to receive. My grandfather left the fruits of his life's work to me, and I'd like to put that to good use. The Children's Hospital and clinics are just the beginning of what we could do."

"I love your ideas," Juliana said. "My specialty is spreading the word, so I think we'd make a good team."

Henri hugged her close to his side. "That's the best part of all."

Juliana loved hearing that. During their sail, they'd had long talks on the boat after the girls had gone to bed. Once he'd confided his most intimate secrets to her, their relation-ship had quickly advanced to a new level of trust and intimacy, though they'd maintained separate staterooms with the girls on board. Their most intimate expression of love could wait, they agreed, though it was growing increasingly difficult. Juliana observed the customs of her faith, and he respected that.

"I meant to tell you," Juliana added. "I received a call before I left the boarding house. Your new Chateau Laurent wine labels are ready. I can pick them up for you tomorrow."

"Let's go together. I can hardly wait to see how they've turned out. You really elevated the design Solange began. I know she would have been thrilled." Henri rubbed her hand as he spoke. "We can have lunch on the pier. I know a place that has the best garlic crab and oysters Rockefeller."

Juliana groaned with her hand on the stomach. "Cioppino, Chinese food, albacore, clam chowder, sourdough bread... Are you seducing me with food again?"

"You bet. With food... and wine. Speaking of which..." Henri stopped at a vine to inspect the small, tight grapes, the berries of the vine.

"The leaves and fruit are already turning," Juliana said. The rich burnished color was a signal that harvest was imminent.

"These cabernet berries are bursting with life and vigor." Henri popped a couple of grapes into his mouth and handed her a few. "Consider the promise the cabernet grape holds within its fruit, the transformation it undergoes, and the witness it will be to celebrations, good friends, and love." His eyes crinkled in a smile. "Especially for us."

"I'd like that." She tasted the grapes. "These will make fine wine. It's going to be a phenomenal vintage this year. I can feel it."

"So, you do have intuitive powers, just as the woman in Chinatown said."

"I'm predicting many good things this year," she said with a wink.

Henri squinted in the sunlight of a cloudless sky. "If this warm weather keeps up, we might have an early harvest this year. And now that we have labels, we can start bottling the wine that's been aging in barrels."

"Have more orders come in?" Since they'd returned, the gala and the press coverage of the event had spurred interest. Both of them had been inundated by calls from collectors, hotels, and wine shops.

Henri laughed. "I've taken so many orders I might have to put the girls to work. You've been spectacular at generating interest in Chateau Laurent wines."

"Your wine speaks for itself. I just gave it a nudge in the right direction."

"That was some kind of nudge." Frowning, Henri said, "Don't discount what you've done."

Juliana laughed. "I'm *not* discounting my work. You haven't received my bill yet." She loved teasing him.

"Uh-oh, how about a special discount?"

"Are you kidding? After what you put me through, I should charge you double."

"Me? What about you?" Henri's eyes were sparkling.

They both started laughing, and Henri picked her up and swung her around. Juliana threw her head back, drinking in the pure joy of the moment. One day at a time, that's how she had decided to live with Henri. Considering the heartbreak she'd been through with Alfonso and the tragedies Henri had survived, she'd learned to never take anything for granted.

Henri set her on her feet, and she touched her lips to

his. "I'm glad you're feeling more relaxed today, Henri." Just as he'd promised her, he had seen the doctor she'd told him about in nearby Sonoma. After only a few visits, his hyper-vigilance seemed to have eased. He'd told her he'd been sleeping a little better, though the therapy process would take time. They had even talked about sending Anne and Beatrice to school, much to the girls' delight.

"That's because you have a funny effect on me, Miss Cardona. Someday, I'll wear down your defenses."

"I wasn't aware I had any defenses left."

"Oh, but you do," he said, his voice deep with desire. Henri twirled her around as he had when they'd danced the night of the gala. Dipping her low to the ground, he held her gaze. "But you're worth waiting for, my darling. Someday soon, I plan to carry you over our threshold."

Her heart in her throat, she asked, "Is that a proposal?"

"As a matter of fact, it is." He swung her up to face him, and then he dropped to one knee before her. "I would be honored to be your husband."

Juliana was sure he could hear her heart pounding, and she hardly trusted her voice. Yet, she drew a breath, pursed her lips, and put a hand on her hip. "You're too late. Anne and Beatrice already proposed on your behalf in the letter they sent me."

He blinked. "I swear I didn't put them up to it."

"It was our secret." Extending her hands, Juliana reached out to him and brought him to his feet.

"I'll take that as yes," he said, whirling her around.

"Yes, yes, yes," she cried, laughing between the kisses he showered on her face.

The End

Note from Jan

Thank you for reading *Life is a Cabernet*, and I hope you enjoyed this novella. If you'd like to remain in beautiful Napa Valley and journey to Tuscany, Italy, *The Winemakers* is the sweeping saga of Juliana's best friend, Caterina, whose family secrets threaten to destroy the winery and everyone they love.

You might also like to read *Seabreeze Inn*, a contemporary beach series about two sisters and a historic beach inn. Or if you've read that, return to the shores of Summer Beach in *The Coral Cottage*. Join three sisters as they each seek haven in the family beach house with their wonderfully eccentric grandmother and recreate their lives.

To hear about my new releases, please join my VIP Readers Club. Thank you very much for reading.

More to Explore

If you like historical novels set by the sea, you'll want to savor *The Chocolatier*. Be whisked away into a fascinating world on the gorgeous Italian coast of Amalfi, where a newly widowed chocolatier from San Francisco discovers a mysterious secret. Between chocolate tastings and fabulous 1950s styles and music, this was one of my favorite books to research.

Another of my favorite novels is *Hepburn's Necklace*, set in beautiful Lake Como, Italy. Find out what happens when a costume designer discovers a necklace that Audrey Hepburn gave her great-aunt—and the long-buried secret its discovery reveals. If you like *Roman Holiday*, you can relive the film in this romantic saga.

If you like World War II sagas, *Scent of Triumph* is about a courageous young French perfumer torn between two continents, who strives to escape the past and reunite her family. It's a feast for the senses, with a story for those who love heart-wrenching sagas.

And if you enjoy reading contemporary series, look for my *Love California* collection of linked, standalone books, beginning with *Flawless*. Meet a group of devoted friends and their romantic interests, and join them on their world-wide adventures—beginning with a trip to Paris. My love of travel inspired these stories, so get your literary passport ready.

ABOUT THE AUTHOR

Jan Moran is a *USA Today* bestselling author of stylish, uplifting, and emotionally rich contemporary and 20th-century historical women's fiction.

A few of her favorite things include a fine cup of coffee, dark chocolate, fresh flowers, laughter, and music that touches her soul. An avid traveler, Jan draws inspiration from locales steeped in history. She lives near the beach in southern California and is originally from Austin, Texas.

Most of her books are available as audiobooks, and her historical fiction is widely translated into German, Italian, Polish, Dutch, Turkish, Russian, Bulgarian, Romanian, Portuguese, and Lithuanian, among other languages.

If you enjoyed this book, please consider leaving a brief review online for your fellow readers where you purchased this book, or on Goodreads.

To read Jan's other novels, visit www.JanMoran.com.

ACKNOWLEDGMENTS

Life is a Cabernet was written during the summer in which I said *au revoir* to my mother, Jeanne Fuller Hollenbeck, who shared so many memories of her life during World War II and the twentieth century with me. This was the last book I read to her. So I must say, "Thank you, Mama, for urging me to keep writing. *Besos.*"

Deep gratitude to my family: my son, Eric; my daughter-law, Ginna; my granddaughter, Zoe; my brother, Mike; my nephews Mitch and Justin; and Michelle. Thank you all for sharing the love in our family.

Made in the USA
Middletown, DE
28 July 2023

35875478R00066